BONESY'S WOLF
WATCHING SERVICE

Bonesy's Wolf Watching Service

R.W. KENDALL

Chapter 1

Weird, I Thought That I Was Dead

Being dead was very easy, so easy that I can't remember any of it. There are bits and pieces, I think, that set in. It may be my imagination though, I can not be sure.

Dying sucked.

I can't recommend it at all. Terrible stuff. It took me a while to remember that, but we'll get to it later on in the story. I would like to write this as authentically as I can, and remembering things when you are a re-animated corpse of sorts is fuzzy at best. It comes in waves. I mean, at first I remembered nothing. I imagine it is how a child feels when they fall asleep and someone moves them. You wake up in an unfamiliar place and have no idea where you are or what is going on at all.

By and by, thoughts sneak into your mind that you believe connect with you. Words, pictures, memories. But, they are just pieces of things.

For example, when I was first reanimated, I glanced at one of the little skeletons beside me and thought, "Goblin." I did not know what that word meant. Later on I knew, but at that moment, no clue.

I hated the goblin, which was strange, because not only did I not know what a Goblin was, I did not know what hate was. I just wanted it not near me and maybe destroyed.

These were also concepts foreign to me then, although I learned them in time as well.

Let's pop back a bit, though, to what I remembered first.

I was dead. And as I have said before, I remember none of it. It was great. I know that there are a lot of people out there wondering what it is like to be dead, especially for a long period, but I got nothing for you in that department. Like I said, I sometimes think there are bits and pieces there, kind of like when you wake from a dream and you can remember a bit, but then it is gone almost instantly.

Anyway, I'm laying there minding my own business. A pile of bones in a cave. When all of a sudden I see this green mist all around me. The door to the room I am in is rising and this mist just wrapped around my skull and bones. My head rises and connects to my other bones. At least I think that they are mine. I never thought about that until now, as I write this. Could be anyone who was in that cave when they died bones. That is a bit hard to take, but I guess it does not matter much.

The bones are mine now either way.

I noticed a ring upon my finger (I did not know it was a ring, but it was shiny with an engraving of a dragon on it. This does not matter much in this story, but may later on) I also noticed that a belt with a sword and scabbard loosely tied around my waist. This had the same dragon on the hilt as well.

As my bones formed my body, I looked around and saw that some of the other skeletons (skels; I decided to call them later) were about my size. Some were four-legged, and some were smaller. These smaller ones made me think of the word "goblin," which brought potent feelings that I was not ready to feel yet.

I reached for my sword to strike at one of the goblins, but my belt fell to my feet. Apparently, your waist is a lot smaller without muscle. Or fat. Or skin. I pulled my belt up and tightened it a bit, then went to strike out at the goblin when a voice called out, "come."

Looking towards the sound, my feet and legs involuntarily started walking towards the door and a man there. He wore some robes that, at one time, were probably quite extravagant. Now they looked worn and tired. The man looked familiar, but being newly not so dead, I couldn't place him. I thought to call out "Hoy

Jeff. How have you been?" But there were three distinct problems with doing so:

1. I didn't know how or even if I could speak at the time.
2. No one else that had arisen in the cave was calling out to Jeff. This could be that they did not know Jeff, or were just acquaintances of Jeff. They just seemed to be falling in line the best they could and walking towards where Jeff was. None of them seemed to look in any direction but Jeff's and I began to think, for the first time, that I was the only one of us that was thinking "what the hell is going on?"
3. I did not know if his name was Jeff.

Turns out (we'll see this later in the story) his name was not Jeff. I am uncertain where that name came from, but until we get to a bigger reveal of who Jeff actually is, I am going to continue to refer to him as Jeff, because that is what I did at the time. Don't worry, dear reader, I will be certain to indicate who Jeff is later.

I decided that I should just get in line with the other skels and try not to draw attention to myself. I may have a slight recognition of Jeff, but that did not mean that he was friend or foe. Just that I recognized him.

We marched on and followed him out of the cave and through a maze. We ended up outside a mountain that wound its way down into a valley. It was a long walk. I would describe the walk, but that would bore you. I have read things where they describe the long walk, with little interaction along the way, and those books had bored me greatly, so I will spare you. If you want a story about a long, boring walk with very little interaction here and there, and then another long, boring walk, I'd read another book if I were you.

I noticed that Jeff had left us. I'm not sure where or when he did, because I wasn't paying much attention. My body was still forced to walk, but my mind was not forced to pay attention. When I noticed him missing, I looked all around, but could not find him. I asked a skel, but he was no help at all. At some point, though, Jeff had been replaced with a skel who had armor on.

I was a bit jealous of this skel. I hadn't noticed until then that I was naked except for my belt with the sword, but there I was. Naked as a baby.

Well, a skinless baby.

I wanted that armor. Why should this skel have armor and I not have even the simplest of cloaks? It didn't seem very fair at all. But it was what it was. He had armor and I, unfortunately, did not. I was sad (although I did not quite know that yet. Sad was new to me. I would understand it well as time went on.)

We marched on, and without Jeff to discourage me, I tried to interact with those around me. Not the goblins, ick, but the human-sized ones. I said things like "how's it going today?" and "Nice weather, huh?" you know small talk and what not, but got no response. At one point, I thought one skeleton was trying to speak, but he was just falling over. I felt funny saying "Hmmm?" to him, when he fell, but I guess no one else noticed as the skeleton behind him just walked right over him.

I even tried to get the attention of one of the four-legged skels, attempting a whistle (impossible with no lips, being bored I tried many times) and saying "here boy," but got nothing.

We walked through the woods for what felt like forever, but I never got tired, it seemed like I should have, until we reached a clearing.

Through the clearing, I saw a wondrous sight. I saw a wondrous sight of hundreds of skels gathered and shooting arrows from bows over and over. They flew like rain on the plain, landing at various distances. Then they just shot again, over and over.

For a quick moment, it seemed like the control over me had gone away and I was free to explore. I walked towards the side and watched the skels shoot. Many of the armored skels seemed to lead the others. I thought about running, but having no real clue where I was, this did not make much sense, so I stayed with my pack.

As we stood there and I watched the arrows fly from the hilltop. I didn't know why we were just sitting around, but none of the other skels seemed to mind, so I just sat on the grass and watched the festivities. It was actually a relaxing way to spend the day, and it seemed like everyone had forgotten about us.

I was rooting for one skel. It (I couldn't tell if it was male or female, but I didn't think it mattered much in this form) wasn't shooting too well. Every now and again, an arrow would launch a great distance, but most plinged just a few feet. I was rooting it on, at some points audibly, but I thought that unwise for the most part. Bringing as little attention to myself seemed to be the way to go, as my silent compatriots were.

They just stood there, unmoving. They seemed to watch, but no reaction was detectable. They just stood staring into the valley. I was confused and bored. But the skels stared on, and really, I had nowhere to go. I seemed not to tire at all. It was like tired wasn't a thing to us skels.

Anyway, this one skel that I was rooting on kind of failed with the bow. I watched as an armored one came towards it. A sense of unease washed over me as I realized none of the armored ones had ever come this close to any other. It kept shooting, sometimes out into the field, but mostly just a few feet. I watched on, willing the thing to just shoot better, more consistently.

It didn't.

At one point, the armored one raised its hand and said something, although the word didn't carry to me. Two four-legged skels came from the trees in a rush. The skel kept shooting, unaware of the four-legged skels, their large skulls, their large teeth.

It kept shooting even as the four-leggers (wolves was the word that came into my mind) ripped it apart.

It kept trying to shoot as the wolves tore the bones apart. I could hear the cracking. The skel was unphased as the wolves crushed its bone to dust. Its legs were gone, its pelvis broken. Its arms tried to grip the bow as the wolves destroyed it piece by piece. It continued to shoot from the ground, half a skel. It kept going.

The two wolves finished with the lower half and took the skull. Crushing it between their jaws. It was just a rib cage and two arms. The wolves kept coming.

As I watched from my hilltop, knowing that I would probably be shooting my own bow soon. Knowing that I had no recourse if Jeff said to shoot.

The wolves kept coming.

Until the end, being just hands and arms, it still kept trying to shoot.

Chapter 2

Somebody's Watching Me

We watched for what seemed like an eternity. I wished I could have slept, but at least I could move around, watch, sit, laid down for a bit. The rest of the squad just stood there.

I started wondering why I seemed to be the only one who was self-conscious. Waving my hand in front of a few of them, to no effect. I touched one, but that seemed to be a bad idea. It grabbed me and I think if I continued the encounter, it would have ended badly for me.

I think I had been there for about three days, contemplating life, the universe, and everything else that a newly reanimated skeleton could contemplate. Talking to my skel friends (they were brilliant listeners, but not so great at giving advice. They never interrupted me though) and whether I should just be on my way. Seemed strange at the time that I had never even

thought about just leaving. I had just seemed compelled to stay. Then an armored skel appeared through
the trees.

I had been lying about daydreaming, so his sudden
appearance gave me a bit of a shock. "Come," it said,
sounding almost identical to Jeff. Was he talking
through them? Could he see through them? Could he
see through me?

That would be weird. Freaked me out a little just
thinking about it.

Apparently, no one was looking through me as I
tried to get myself back in line as fluidly as possible.

It wasn't fluid.

Far from fluid.

I knocked a poor skel over, apologizing profusely to
something that seemed unaware that it had even fallen
over, lost a foot, and kept falling over because of the
missing foot. I kind of just fell into line and avoided
looking towards the footless skel after trying to give
him his foot back.

As we walked, I saw that he (or she) had figured it
out, limping around without the foot. I gave a half-
hearted thumbs-up and tried to smile, which is also
quite difficult without lips.

Fearing that the skel was doomed and feeling bad for
him as I remembered what happened to that other skel
with the bow. There wasn't much I could do about it at
the moment.

It was our turn.

The armored skel led us to where we would be shooting. I hoped I would be good at it. These others seemed to not know what was going on, but I did. What if I got destroyed and still knew what was happening around me, unable to move or interact? This thought haunted me as I thought of sitting there for eternity just watching, well, nothing mostly, go by.

I needed to do well.

In the end, I had not needed to worry. I was great! Missing foot guy wasn't bad either. It took him a minute to get his balance, but he was shooting like a pro in no time. Did better than me on some shots. It was incredibly boring. Arrow after arrow, I shot through the field. I timed myself with the others, since every-one was shooting at the simultaneously.

I must have done this before when living, because I was a natural. My arrows flew high and straight, unlike many of my group mates. A wave of sadness washed over me as I observed a few of them being mercilessly shredded by skel-wolves, yet they showed no signs of concern. Still trying to shoot as their bones crunched under their jaws.

It occurred to me that I may have known some of these skels in my life-time. Since we had died in the same spot, we might have died at the same time. I may even had known some of the goblins.

Maybe they had killed me?

That made a bit of sense as to why I wouldn't like them much. Maybe we had been in some great war.

Goblins versus humans. Maybe for generations. Maybe I had fought one to the death. A grand final battle.

Probably not, though.

We were in some weird cavern with treasures around. We most likely were just fighting over gold or something. Idiotic. Jeff might know. I'd have to ask him if I saw him again. I wondered if he would remember me if I talked to him. Or, if I had known him at all. I wondered what his name actually was.

An errant arrow flew from my bow in my day-dreaming daze, hitting an armored skel. The arrow stuck out of his armor. He seemed ok and not to have noticed it at all. But then another armored skel came up to me!

Crap, I thought, thinking I had screwed this up.

He'd call over the skel-wolves and I would be dust in no time. I thought to run, but that wasn't happening. I told my legs to move, but nope. Nothing.

The wolves would come soon. "Come" It sounded like Jeff.

I came. I didn't want to, didn't even try to move, but that didn't matter. My body just followed the armored skel without my will.

I felt at least a little relieved that wolves weren't just let loose on me, but of course, this may be a worse fate. We reached a small clearing, and I saw what was going on. It appeared that I had passed the Bow and Arrow test! My armored friend stopped in front of me, picked up a sword and handed it to me. Apparently, he didn't notice that I already had one on my belt. I thought about saying something, but thought again. What would be the point?

"Destroy" and he pointed.

On the other side of the small clearing, another skel was receiving his sword. His handler was pointing at me. Something impelled me to destroy the other skel as it began running, full-speed, at me. No regard for its safety at all. Although I knew I would have to follow orders, it did seem that I had some will and could decide how to destroy my opponent myself. I could not run away, as I realized from the days on the hill, but I didn't have to leave myself defenseless.

My opponent had surprising speed, reaching me much quicker than I suspected, but I parried his sword with ease. He turned with quickness, but again my sword blocked the attack.

As he continued to charge me and I continued to avoid his blows, I surveyed some of the other battles. They were quick.

I mean extremely quick.

The two skels would rush at each other and try to deliver a blow. Whoever did the most damage first won. Soon, there were many broken skels, still trying to fight being crushed by their opponent. It seemed pointless to destroy this many of your army (is that what we were? If we were, I might be in a load of trouble. All these things knew of was to rush and smash.) Meanwhile, I kept dodging and parrying until the skel tried to stab me instead of crush me.

Its sword got jammed in between two of my ribs and it came loose from his hand. It ran at me again, without his sword and I again dodged him, this time striking his spine as he went by... He fell, now in two. Both halves trying to continue the fight. The legs tried to kick at me, which I found funny, since they were way too far away to have any chance of hitting.

The arms dragged the rest of the body to me. Before I knew it, the sword swung. I thought the battle was over at that point, but I couldn't stop.

"Destroy." I heard again as the sword struck downward.

I had no control.

"Destroy." Jeff's voice in my head. Again, the sword struck.

My mind left my body. it had no purpose there any way. I had no control. There was nothing I could do.

"Destroy." The image, the helpless feeling, even today, has never left my mind.

"DESTROY."

I continued to smash the skel in front of me. It had stopped moving many minutes ago, but I kept smashing.

It was nothing but dust. It had stopped moving a while ago. Well, except for its foot, or maybe just a toe, but it was far from me. I still moved towards it. I did not want to, but I did. I took my great sword and smashed the toe.

Nothing else moved. I could stop.

After the sword, well fight may be a strong word, but that is all I got right now. We kind of just sat around what seemed to be a makeshift village. I can not say that it disappointed me at all, though. I needed a break after all that had happened the last few days. For a bit, I just sat and wished for sleep.

Sleep did not come.

I thought, when I was alive the first time (if you can call whatever this as being 'alive' the second time) that being sent into the Seven Hells would be all demons torturing your soul and messed up stuff like that. But, at this point, I felt that this was my punishment, and Jeff was the Devil himself.

The boredom and inability to just leave would have been bad enough on its own. Add the fruitless attempts at interaction with the other skels and being ignored as if I was not even there.

Then the inability to just shut off my brain (as it were) and sleep.

Even when I contemplated (not too seriously, but after a few weeks it did begin to seep into my mind that I must find a way out somehow) destroying myself. Unfortunately, I did not know if I'd just be a sentient pile of dust.

Everyone else just stood around doing nothing. Waiting for something to happen. Some order to be given. They did not seem to mind at all, so why did I? Why was I this special one who had to endure this torture?

I tried to entertain myself, sure. Antagonizing a few skels, striking up a conversation, but they only reacted if I seemed to be a threat.

I drew things in the dirt for a while. One was pretty good and was getting large until a group of armored skels trampled over it on their way to the fighting grounds.

I watched some battles, but these things were just so stupid. They'd run at each other and smash each other, and then one or both would be crushed down and destroyed. It was old before I even started watching.

I was hoping to find one, just one, skel that showed any sign of knowing what was going on. But never did.

Time got a little messy. I just stopped paying attention to it for the most part. So I would have to say maybe a few weeks in, I saw something in the woods, watching. Thinking, at first, that it was just some animal, I dismissed it. But I saw it again later that day. I started towards it and it ran. A two-legged, small creature.

The goblin word came to me again. I thought that it was just my mind losing the plot for a bit, but a few days later I saw another. And another.

Then a few more.

I thought about maybe telling one of the armored skels what I saw, but I did not think that they would listen to me. And besides, I thought, it might break up some of this monotony if the goblin things did decide to do something. So I kept it to myself.

In my mind, they were scouting us, looking for a place to either attack or steal from. Figuring in the fact that we had no supplies or food, I was guessing an attack of some sort was correct. Although I was not in the mood to kill anything, some sort of attack or something would break up the day a bit. Give me something else to do, at least.

Chapter 3

Battle Fog

Eventually, they did attack. Although they took their sweet time getting around to it. I started thinking that it was all just a tease, and that they were just watching us going about our boring daily lives.

I could not understand it. They continued to watch as we did nothing. More and more of them came. At least I think it was more and more. Maybe I was just more aware of them and they were there the whole time. Either way, they did not seem to be much of a threat. They were only about three feet tall or something, with little clubs. They had wolves, though. But so did we.

To me, they seemed to just be little savages, not understanding what they were seeing.

I was wrong. I would not find out just how wrong I was until later, but they knew what they were seeing and were biding their time, waiting for the right opportunity to strike.

Something else was up with us as well. No, no one said anything to me, but the armored skels were moving around a bit more and were gathering groups of skels into various areas. It seemed we were being put into battalions or something. They brought me into one group and I admired the goblins' patience.

If they were to attack, we were now sitting ducks all grouped together. I cursed my predicament, as I was pretty sure we were going to get ambushed and wiped out. Being in the group closest to where I saw the goblins did not help me feel better at all, so I tried to stay as far away as I could.

I made a few passing remarks to try to warn the others, but they paid me no mind. Gripping my sword and backing against a wall, I waited. It would come soon. I was not quite sure how I knew it was coming soon. I could not see any movement just then. A nervous excitement filled me, though. I just seemed to expect the action coming.

I did not anticipate where it would begin, however. It came from behind me, not the front. An explosion rumbled under my feet as I saw rubble fly over head.

Then another, and another.

"Destroy the intruders." Filled my head, and I assume all the others got the same command as well because they started scurrying towards the trees to meet the goblins.

One goblin came running full speed right towards me, and I drew my sword. It had a powder keg on its back with a lit fuse. "Destroy" came into my head, but I somehow ignored it, maybe because I had realized that this one was about to destroy itself.

I swung my sword and swatted it to the side and ran towards the woods. It struck the building and fell. Then exploded.

If I had been flesh and bone, I would have been killed on the spot as shrapnel flew through me, but luckily, I was only bone. And none of the projectiles broke any of them. I ran towards the incoming goblins, who took out a few of the lead skels, who had just rushed in with no strategy, with their clubs. I parried the club blows and struck out. Taking a few goblins easily.

What I would have called adrenaline poured into me as I fought and a haze fell around my mind. The only things that I could hear were the sounds of battle and the persistent 'destroy.' The only things I could see were the battlefield and the competitors.

More explosions went off in the distance, back in the village, but I paid no heed. The battle lust was strong.

The goblins, with their main aim complete, fled. I saw one get separated, and I ran towards it, a small one who found opportunity and ran away from the village, but also separated from her pack.

Compelled to destroy, I followed her.

I chased her deep into the woods and the sounds of the battle subsided. The battle fog that had taken over my mind began to fade as well, but the persistent 'destroy' command kept me in my pursuit even after I had tried to command my legs to stop.

I was relieved from time to time when I would lose sight of her and my legs would stop, but then I would see a glimpse, or a track, or hear a noise, and I would be right back on the chase.

As I was chasing, the command seemed to get weaker. I still could not stop myself from the chase, but it was, I guess I would say, duller.

The girl goblin obviously knew the woods here, jumping over fallen trees or crawling under if needed. I felt sad for her since if any of the other skels had been the one that pursued her, she would have been long gone. But she got me.

At one point, she tried to double back around and either flank me or return to her people, but I saw it coming and had to cut her off.

We both paused as I came out about 15 feet in front of her. She looked like a kid. About twelve years old if I was pressed for a guess. We just stood there staring, just waiting for the other to make a first move. At least that is what I was waiting for. For all I knew, she could have been waiting for reinforcements.

I pondered this in my reasoning. I had to destroy her, it seemed, if I could. However; even with my apparent disdain for goblins, it seemed rather uncouth to destroy a 12-year-old girl, or boy even, if that had been the case, no matter the species.

It seemed that I could decide the process in which I attempted to destroy this girl, and I decided to wait until she made a first move. If she had reinforcements, and they somehow prevented me from destroying said girl, that seemed to be okay with my orders. So I waited for her.

And waited.

And waited some more.

She just stared at me for what seemed forever. It probably was only a few minutes, but it seemed like a very long time.

About then I realized that maybe this goblin would understand me if I talked (this revelation came way too late, it seems) and as I began to speak; the girl screamed.

It was the most horrible, primal and actually quite impressive scream I think I have ever heard. I say that even now, remembering my past life for the most part. And even after that moment. Well, there was one more. Later on. But We'll hear that one when we get to it.

Even in my new skel state, I was paralyzed to move after her scream. She turned and ran, and I just stood there for a few moments.

Awe-struck.

Then I followed her off into the woods again.

Her swiftness impressed me, as did my own. I had seen how the other skels had moved. Well, except for the skel wolves, they were quite agile. I was definitely a step above the regular ones, though. Maybe because of my sentience? Maybe. I really did not know at this point. Could have just been that I was less dead than them.

I turned around a tree that I thought she had run behind and saw nothing. Then I felt her club crush against my rib cage.

I heard a crack, but felt no pain. If she had been stronger, or hit in the right place, she would have broken my rib, or worse. With her force though, it just pushed me a little. I turned. She was right next to me, readying to hit me again.

She was too close. I could not resist attacking when the opportunity was so close.

I tackled the girl without thinking and brought her to the ground. She spun out of my grip and rolled a few feet away. I saw the fear in her eyes and knew she only had two choices at this point: run or fight.

I hoped that she would run. Run fast where I could not get to her. If I knew where she was, I would continue to track her unless I got some other order as far as I knew. If she fought, I would have to kill her.

Or her kill me.

Could I even die? I didn't know. What if something destroyed me, crushed me to dust, as I did my first opponent, and I was damned to that spot for eternity? That did not sound good at all.

I didn't know the extent of the control Jeff had on me. If I got far enough away, could I act on my own? Would it be permanent?

I stood and lifted my sword.

She stood and lifted her club. I liked her. She had a fight in her. If she was going down, she was going to make sure I would pay some price. I admired her. I began to move towards her. I tried to resist, but it was no use. My legs stalked her and my arms rose in defense. I was a puppet at this point. The skeleton's voice (Jeff's voice) continued to burn in my thoughts, overwhelming all others.

"Destroy"

I tried to block it out. Think of anything but the command. Having toast and tea. What was toast and tea? I was not sure, but it would be better than someone forcing me to kill someone I did not want to kill.

"Destroy."

I moved closer. "Run" I thought. If she ran, I would chase. I was tireless and may wear her down, but she was small. "Run and hide." I thought.

"Destroy."

She did not run, although she did move to the right and turn a little. She was left-handed. Trying to get some advantage. I liked her more.

"Destroy."

... towards me, raising her club, getting ready...

"Destroy."

... to strike me, crush my bone...

"Destroy!"

.. I blocked it with my sword.

"Destroy!"

... I pushed her to the ground...
"DESTROY!"
... the word, all I could think...
"DESTROY!"
... I raised my sword over her chest.
"DESTROY!"
... "I'm sorry," I managed to speak, what little help that was. A look of true terror came to me from her eyes. I tried to closed my own but could not and brought down my sword. I could not help it. I could not stop it. I could not resist. The master was pulling the strings.

The sword did not strike true. As I went to plunge my sword into this poor young girl, a wolf tackled me, taking me off of her. It pinned me down, drool flowing from its jowls. I tried to force it off, but it was no use. The wolf was too heavy and too strong.

"Hold that thing, Grimmaw." The child said.

I have to admit that it hurt a bit when she called me a thing. Even though I understood why. I was an undead monster, stalking her and, if this Grimmaw wolf hadn't arrived, would have killed her. Then again, it was her and her people who started it. At least from my point of view. But I knew very little.

Was I 'a thing' now?

We sat there, staring at each other. It was very awkward; me being all pinned down by a giant wolf and her looking down on me. Her eyes showed so much expression. "Hi." came from my mouth. It was the only thing I could think of.

Chapter 4

Meeting Grit

That didn't seem to go over well. Her eyes and mouth got small. "Hi" was probably the wrong thing to say to someone you almost stabbed with a sword. I was not good at these social things. To my credit, I have not had a lot of practice since becoming not so dead. The skels provided little in the way of conversation.

"Why did you say that you were sorry?"

This took me by surprise. I thought for a moment. I didn't want a repeat of the 'hi' from before. Then she raised her club. I would say menacingly raised her club, but if you were ever held on the ground by an enormous wolf and a goblin child that was holding a club ready to smash your head in, you would know that the menacingly was implied. "I didn't want to kill you."

"Sure looked like you did."

I explained, in great detail, about how I could not help it. How I woke up from deadness a couple weeks ago (I thought it was, at least, I was and am still, not so good with time.) How I was pretty good with the bow, but great with the sword. And how I destroyed that one skel when I did not want to. I went on, but you have already read these parts, so I will not repeat them here. If you skipped ahead, now would be a great time to go back. It is not very long.

I was rambling quite a bit, and I saw her face soften, then grow impatient, then kind of annoyed as I began recalling me chasing her.

"I know this part. If Grim lets you up, are you going to try to kill me?" I was perplexed by this question. Letting me up was not an option that I thought would be entertained at this point. I thought a bit, thinking that it might not be a good option to let me up. Then again, getting my head smashed in was definitely not a good option. "I don't know." I settled on. I was actually pretty sure that I would, but I thought we might as well give it a go. The wolf could knock me down again if I tried to kill her.

She whistled. The wolf looked at her and preceeded to drool on me again. I would have said it was gross, but I didn't feel it. The girl nodded. The wolf whined. I got more drool. I'm pretty sure that wolf thought that letting me up was about as good of an idea as I did, which was, well, not very. The girl nodded again. The wolf let me up, giving me a very scary growl as it did. More drool.

I was free.

To my surprise, I did not try to kill her. I did not hear the word destroy, so that was good. We heard some goblins rushing through the woods, cheering. Seemed like my side lost. I was happy about that.

"You seem okay now."

"Could be I'm out of range?" I looked around. The wolf was still eying me. I did not blame it one bit. "Thank you."

She looked up at me and smiled. "I never thought a skeleton would ever thank me." She brushed herself off and put her club away. "Or talk to me, for that matter. Didn't know that you could." She patted the wolf. "I'm Grit. Grimmaw, you already met."

I laughed, "I have no idea who I am, but nice to meet you." I was not lying at that point, I did not know who I was then. "I'm not sure many of us can speak at all."

"I guess you'll go back now."

"Back?" I rubbed the back of my neck, thinking there was a crink or something there. There was not. "Back where?"

She went to the wolf. "Home, with your people." I looked at her and tilted my head. "The other skele-tons."

"Oh, no." I shook my head, and I shrugged my shoulders. "They're not my people. That's not home."

"Where will you go then?"

"I do not know."

Grit sat down across from me for a while. I was wondering what it was she was doing, but she just sat and looked at me. Grimmaw eventually sat as well, and to my surprise, took a nap. I laughed a bit when the wolf snored.

"Won't your people be worried about you?" I said, trying to break the silence.

"Probably, but we're not far." She said back, "Which is why we felt the need to attack."

"Makes sense."

She looked at me for a while longer, seemingly trying to decide something. I was not sure if she was waiting for me to leave or not, but as I had told her, I really had nowhere to go. I was not sure, even though the 'destroy' command had gone away, if I could go anywhere.

"I have a place, I think, at least temporarily."

It had been a while, and I had kind of forgotten what we were talking about. "A place for what?"

"For you to go."

"Oh." I said. She looked at me like that was obvious. "I didn't know that was what we were waiting for."

"No bother, let's go." and she got up. Grimmaw stirred, gave me a quick growl, and followed the girl.

"Wait, where are we going?" I tried to keep up.

"To Old Man Wilkens." She said in her 'that should have been obvious' tone.

"Who?"

"Does it matter?"

I thought on this a second, then said, "Well, a little. Is he going to try to smash me with a club?"

"Probably not, he's blind. If you pretend you're alive, he'll have no idea that you're a skeleton." She stopped and turned to me. "If you hurt him, I will hurt you."

I looked at her, believing every word, "I will do my best."

"Make sure that you do."

"Won't the other, err, goblins, see me?"

"He lives away from the village in a hut. He watches the wolves during the day."

"You have an old blind man watching the wolves?"

"Well, yeah. They did not need much watching until you skeletons... sorry, the skeletons came by. They watch themselves for the most part. A few have been disappearing lately, though." She looked at me. "Maybe you can help."

"Maybe."

"I'll get you some gloves and a cloak. Maybe boots." She looked at my feet. "Zrakkon may have a pair big enough."

"Zrakkon?"

"My cousin. Kind of like my big brother now."

"Oh." I did not know why this goblin, who I had just tried to kill, was helping me. She probably felt pity for me, which made me feel bad. And uncomfortable. But again, I had no other option than to just wander off on my own. I was sure that I would not be welcomed many places, being a skel and all.

"He's big for a goblin, should be a close fit. Then at least you can try to fit in if anyone sees you."

I looked at myself, and then at her. "I don't think that I'm fitting in either way."

"Not at all. But at least you won't freak everyone out right at the get go." She laughed at this. I couldn't help but to laugh as well. It was my first genuine laugh since becoming not so dead.

We got to Old Man Wilken's place, and she told me to wait in the woods for a bit. I looked around the property. Small stone walls ran around the lush green field. Over the hill was a wondrous view of a crystal clear lake. I could stare at it for hours on end.

Grit came back with a long cloak that could not have been worn by a goblin and gloves that slid over my boney fingers. I placed my ring outside the glove, which, to my surprise, actually looked good.

"He said that he'll take you in until I talk to my grandfather."

"Who's your grandfather?"

"The shaman, he'll decide if you can stay."

"What if he doesn't?"

She thought for a moment. "Well, most likely he'll just banish you."

That I was alright with, but she continued.

"It's possible that he'll send a bunch of warriors to destroy you." She shrugged at the last part and went on her way.

Chapter 5

How to Start a Wolf Watching Service

To my surprise, Old Man Wilkens was not a goblin. I can not, one-hundred percent, say he was human, but he definitely was not a goblin. I mean, I am pretty sure he was human, but how do you ask that? Later I met elves of all sorts, dwarfs, half-men, and gnomes, among others, but he seemed to be mostly human, at the very least.

It didn't really matter all that much, as he died about a week after I moved in. No, I didn't kill him, if that's what you were thinking. He just didn't wake up one day.

Overall, I liked him. He was quite pleasant and always offered me food. I always took it and found a way of getting rid of it without him noticing. I tried to eat it once, hoping that maybe, just maybe, I could taste it as it spilled down my bones. No luck though. No taste and just a messy cloak.

I felt that in my before dead life I must have loved food (I was right about this) which made me at least try.

It had been a few days since Grit had left me. A few goblins had come and gone, leaving or picking up wolves. It did not seem like Old Man Wilkens, who I learned was actually Odem, but the goblins had thought that he said Old Man and he decided not to correct them, really did anything.

The goblins would tell him who they were dropping off or picking up. He'd say "Uh, yeah" and pretend to write something down, and they would go with or without a wolf.

Once in a while, the wolf would not be there and he would pretend to look at his list and shrug. Then the goblin would leave. Usually upset. I watch this go on for about a week.

Eventually, I just waited for Odem to fall asleep and I went out to watch the wolves. They were skittish or down right aggressive towards me at first, but then they got used to me being there and settled down some.

One night, I saw what was happening to the wolves who were disappearing. I was walking out among them after Odem had fallen asleep and saw one go running out past the rock walls. They were set up in a maze, which, for the most part, kept the wolves inside the field. This one had seen something and ran out of the walls. They were something like three foot walls that the wolves could easily jump over, they just usually didn't.

Unless they had a reason to.

This one had reason in a small 'bunny' that was running side to side just beyond the last wall. I followed it to investigate.

There was a small pack of humans inside the tree line, moving what appeared to be a stuffed rabbit side to side. When the wolf finally went close enough, I saw the humans pounce. The poor wolf had no chance. Two arrows struck it almost immediately and them three humans attacked with swords.

I decided that my best course of action was to run back towards the Odem's hut as there was not really much I could do for that wolf. I felt bad, but maybe I could help the others. If I went after this one, I was easily outnumbered by six or seven.

The next morning, Odem was dead.

He just never woke up. I shook him a few times, but got no response. I began digging a grave soon after, not knowing what else I could do.

And, of course, later that day, Grit returned.

With her grandfather.

"What the Hells did you do?"

I was definitely not expecting this. I had earlier found one of the two people that I had any real interaction in my not so dead life that did not treat me as either non-existent or an enemy dead, and the other was now attacking me. Grit pounced on me, knocking me over and in all this, dislodging my arm.

"I told you what I would do!" She yelled.

I tried to put my two arms up to block her blows, but this was much less effective without one of them. It did move, to its favor, but it was nowhere near where it should have been. Basically useless, it was. "I did not kill him." I yelled.

This actually worked better than I thought it would. At least she stopped hitting me. I would not say it was good in any way. For now she was crying uncontrollably.

"He just didn't wake up this morning." I said and tried to comfort her with my one attached arm. I did giggle a bit as I saw my other arm trying to hug nothing. I hoped that I could put it back on, though.

"What happened?" The older goblin asked. We had attracted a small crowd of three or four around us now. I felt that it may now be a trial at this point. I began at the best place, the beginning. Then they told me that they already knew the whole story up to about when I met Grit and that I should maybe start with this morning. I said that I thought that may be a good idea. Then I did.

"I went out to watch the sunrise over the lake, as I had been doing the last few days. Usually, Odem..." I was cut off by one of the goblins that I did not know. He raised his hand as if to ask a question.

"Odem." I repeated. I felt this may answer his question. I was wrong.

"Who's Odem?" Grit asked.

"The old man."

"His name is Odem?"

"Yes. Well, was, I guess, now." This got me a stern look.

"That makes more sense." Grit said through the stern look.

"Yes." I said again and waited for someone else to ask a question. They did not, so I continued. "So I saw the humans..." I did not get very far.

"Humans?" the grandfather asked. I was a little perturbed by being interrupted, but then I remembered how Grit had said something about the grandfather maybe ordering my destruction, and held my non existent tongue.

"Yes. I think you have a human, well, infestation." I did not know how to explain it any other way. "I think they are killing your missing wolves."

"Think."

"Well, no, I saw them."

"SAW them?" He asked.

"Yes, over yonder." I pointed. Grit cleared her throat. That was when I realised that I was pointing with my detached arm. In the wrong direction. I corrected this with my currently attached arm.My arm, by this point, had made it back to me and I picked it up, placing it where it should go. To my relief, it seemed to stay put.

"So, I was a bit distracted by the humans." I continued, "I did not notice the smell."Grit gave me a sour look, "Smell?"

"More of a 'lack' of smell. No coffee."

"Coffee?" someone asked. I was not sure who it was at this time. There seemed to be a lot of goblins gathering around us now. Knowing that they weren't entirely fond of my kind, it was a bit uncomfortable.

"Yes, Odem..."

"Who's Odem?" someone yelled in the back.

"Old Man Wilkens," someone else yelled, "Keep up!"

"I just got here!" He yelled back.

"Sorry, I'll fill you in later." The other said.

I waited for all this to subside. I certainly did not want to be rude to those who may want to destroy me. They seemed to all be sitting around me now, though, so I felt at least a wee bit safe to continue.

"Yes, so Odem..."

"That's the old man." Someone yelled. I decided not to engage.

"Yes, he makes, er, made coffee every morning. We would share a cup."

"How do you drink? You're a skeleton." Someone yelled.

"Shh!" another yelled. "Save questions for later!" The sheer number of goblins who had gathered around at this point was unbelievable. I had no idea where they were even coming from.

I tried to remember what it was I was talking about, having completely lost track of the entire situation. But I then looked at the shovel on the ground. That righted the ship. "Ah, yes. So I smelled no coffee. Which was not normal. I went to check on him and he was not breathing. So I decided to bury him."

This seemed to disappoint the goblin crowd that had formed. I think mainly because it was quite anti-climatic. I wanted to give them a bit more of a grand story, but that was about it.

They continued to stare at me, waiting for more. I felt as if I had let them down a bit, but it was the logical end of the story. Then I remembered. "Would you like to see where I saw the humans?"

The goblins, although not entirely enthusiastic, de-cided that yes, they did indeed want to see where I had seen the humans. And so I took them.

The oldest (I assumed he was Grit's grandfather be-cause they had come together. On this point I was correct, but we had not been introduced properly yet) walked next to me to the outskirts of trees where I had seen the humans. I showed them telltale signs of a struggle and even found some remnants of rabbit fur lying about.

"Six or seven, you said?" He asked me.

"That's how many I saw."

"Missed two." He moved a little deeper into the woods.

"Well, it was dark. And they were moving about all willy-nilly. And..."

He stopped me by raising his hand toward my face. "It's not your fault."

That calmed me a bit. I wasn't sure why I was so nervous around him. I mean, the whole getting destroyed by all these goblins was part of that for sure, but something about the old man just made you not want to disappoint him. "How do you know?"

He just pointed up. There were two sets of paths up the tree made with some sort of metal climbing spikes or claws. They were fresh markings.

"Nice eye." I said.

"You get used to seeing these things with age and experience." He raised his hand to his scraggled beard and massaged his chin. He was about to say something when a rather large goblin tackled me out of the blue, yelling something about stealing his boots.

I tumbled. A toe seemed to dislodge inside one of the said boots. I was pretty sure it had come off and hoping that I could replace it as easily as I did my arm. I was not happy about this turn of events, having been tackled two too many times today already, and still, I thought, having to finish digging a grave.

"Give me my damned boots!" He said, quite angrily. I was also in an angry mood now, so I rolled with the momentum and tossed him into a rock wall.

This did not make him any less angry at all.

He grabbed my (his?) boot with the dislodged toe in it and pulled hard. A little harder than he had to since they fit a little loose. He, and my toe, (the middle one, which I had grown fond of, as it was a tad longer than all the others. I am pretty sure that it belonged to someone else at one point) went flying. I tried to track my toe's flight, but lost it when the goblin, who I had deduced was Grit's cousin Zrakkon by now, attacked my other boot.

"Give it up Bonesy, you thief."

I laughed to myself, thinking that Bonesy as an insult probably did not come out as insulting as the insulter had imagined it would. I actually kind of liked it. He then hit me in the face with the boot that he did manage to get off. I reached for my sword.

I think that you can imagine, pulling a sword on a goblin in a mass of other goblins who did not know you was a very bad idea. Uncountable, well probably countable, that is a bit of a lie there, but I happened to be too busy at the time to do any counting, weapons emerged. One woman goblin had quite an impressive set of not only foot long hand claws that looked like they could rip the skin off and elephant, but foot claws to match. If I had skin, I would not have wanted to see those coming, that's for sure.

Grit got between me and them. That was good, but they did not actually seem to be standing down any.

She turned to Zrakkon, "I gave him your boots." She said.

This new wrinkle did stop the goblin mob, as did me putting my sword away. To be honest, I wasn't sure if it was my sword being sheathed or the promise of a bit of family drama that made them stop.

After getting to know them (spoiler, I did not get destroyed at this point) I am quite convinced it was the latter. They did like their drama. Especially of the family kind.

Zrakkon was not happy with his cousin, but Grit did not back down. They were in the middle of hashing out something that was probably an old family matter. I understood none of it, since they were talking in a language I did not understand. When they both turned to look at the crowd, which was watching them very intently, they stopped. Zrakkon walked away in a huff.

"Would you like the job?" The grandfather asked me, in the middle of all this. It seemed a weird request, given what had just transpired.

To be honest, he may have been talking to me for a while, but I had zoned him out. The family drama, my poor lost toe, which without the boots, was just drawing attention to itself, or not drawing attention to itself, since it wasn't there. I'm not sure how that works, but I noticed it very much. "What job?"

"Wolf Watcher." He said, "We need one. The last one died."

"I am aware."

"Yes, I guess you are. Well, you can stay here if you watch them."

"Okay" was my answer.

And that is how you start a wolf watching service.

Chapter 6

A Good Boy

I really did not have anywhere else to go at that point, anyway. Except maybe back to the skels. They probably would not even know that I had been gone. Or that I had come back, for that matter. I may have to do all those bow and sword trials again. No, the goblins seemed to be a better option. I had a bit of a friendship with Grit. Her grandfather probably did not fully trust me, but seemed willing to give me a chance. And even Zrakkon gave me a kind of rival, which could be fun.

Most of the goblins did not ignore me, at the very least. Even with those that did, I knew they could hear me. They just chose not to respond.

That's how it seemed to play out. About half of the goblins either liked or tolerated my presence, mostly the children and older female ones. While the other half, older (although none seemed as old as the grandfather) males and the adults either hated or at least disliked me.

There were a few that I could not get a read one, but overall, those were the groups.

None left their wolves with me at first, though. Which was fine with me. Oh, a few came by the field and let the wolves run about, but they did not leave them with me. Probably feeling me out. Some ignored me and some said "Hi Bonesy." and I'd wave back. Guessing that was my name for now, I embraced it. It could have been much worse, I thought.

I could sit around and do nothing, wander about a bit. Watch the lake. Some humans enjoyed the lake one day. They seemed mostly harmless, though. Just swimming about and fishing. They were far enough away from me and the goblins, so no trouble.

That was the day Grit came by with Grimmaw. Time mattered little to me, so I lost track a lot, but I would guess about five days past the double tackle day would be about right.

"Sorry about Zrakkon."

"Not a worry." I waved her off. "Besides, you stood up for me." I also turned my boots towards her. Zrakkon did not seem to really want them, so I kept them. I couldn't find my toe, though. It's a little weird as I could still sense it out there, all alone in the grass. I even wiggled it now and again. Maybe it was my imagination.

"I guess."

"It meant a lot."

Grit turned her head and attention to Grimmaw. "Can you watch him today?"

"That's my job."

"Doesn't look like it." She spread her arms wide to show the extreme lack of wolves under my watch.

I laughed and shrugged my shoulders. It was still my job, even if no one took advantage of it. "Any special instructions?"

"Keep away from humans."

"Got it." We went into my cabin and I found Odem's writing pad. I looked at it, really, for the first time. The old man really had impeccable handwriting. It was like art. Beautiful. I would have felt bad messing up his final sheet with whatever writing I could manage.

I found a blank sheet and a pen by the desk and sat down. I started writing Grimmaw's name. I had no idea what day it was, so I put a one next to it. I guessed that I would just keep track of how many days they stayed by making slash marks. Maybe another method would come to me later. "You don't actually have to keep that if you don't want to. It was more of Old Man's, I mean Odem's, thing."

"I think I'll keep it. Makes me feel official." I puffed out what I had for a chest. Grit laughed. I pushed the paper towards her and held out the pen. "Sign here."

Grit looked at the pen and then down slightly. I got the message.

"Thumb print works." She obliged. "Where are you going?"

"Oh, we're going out to scout..." She stopped mid sentence and looked out towards the lake.

"Skeletons." I finished for her.

"Humans, actually. My grandfather is worried about how close they are from what you told us," she said.

I put my gloved hand on her shoulder as we watched Grimmaw roll around on the tall grass. "First time with humans?"

"Yeah." I could tell that she was nervous.

"You'll be fine. I remember a tale of a young goblin girl surviving a battle with a dashing, quite skilled, and did I say quite a dashing skeleton once." She eased up and relaxed a little and laughed. "Why isn't he going?"

"Grimmaw?" I nodded. "Good killer, not a good scout. He'd attack something."

Looking at the beast roll around, stop, snort, and actually be scared of what appeared to be a large bug hopping in the grass, you would question the killer part. I knew better, of course, but in the field he just wanted to play.

Grit walked down to him, and he ran to her. I watched as she gave him a thorough patting. It was funny to see the giant wolf that had pinned me to the ground not so long ago succumb to the tiny goblin over a simple thing like belly pats. It was too bad they seemed to be caught in between the humans and skels. Without those threats, they may be quite a peaceful bunch.

After Grit left, I sat out with Grimmaw for a bit and threw a stick for him. To my surprise, he went and got it and then ran back to me. So I threw it again. This actually went on for much longer than I thought it would. Quite a mindless activity, but Grimmaw got his exercise, and I got some time out of my head, which was needed.

One time I threw the stick, and the wolf decided not t get it, looked at me a way that could really only be interpreted as 'why the Hells did you do that?' and laid down on the grass.

I wondered for a wee bit why he thought that I would not throw it, when in fact, I had been throwing it for quite some time, but decided it was probably just a wolf thing.

I left Grimmaw to lying on the grass and went into Odem's hut to have a look around. It was quite tidy for a tiny hut that had been owned by a blind man. This is to say that it was not tidy at all, but you could tell that he did make some effort into trying to keep it tidy. I thought to clean it, but then thought that I had no idea how long I would be there and decided to put it off.

I found some more paper. Actually, I found a ton of paper and thought that this may be a good opportunity to write some things down. I'd explain what I decided to write, but since you are reading it, I figure that you already know. So I won't. Grit and the other goblins already got annoyed at me for explaining things that were unnecessary. I feel that I am a quick learner.

Grimmaw came and set with me while I wrote, and was soon snoring.

I guessed at least one being had accepted me and that felt good. Even if it was a wolf. I patted his head and wrote, waiting for Grit to come back, or something else to happen.

Nothing, however, really happened that day. Nor the next. Nor the next. Grit did not even come back, and I began to worry. So did Grimmaw. Well, I guess that I guessed that Grimmaw was worried, because he started acting a bit strange after the second day. No longer was throwing a stick any fun, and he stopped eating as much as usual. He kept a watchful eye on the horizon. He was a good wolf.

I told him so repeatedly. Some old jerky was in one of the draws of the desk so I threw a few to him. The wolf had gobbled them up before, but this time he just looked at them, turn his head and snorted.

Grimmaw made his way outside on the next day, the first that I had seen rain since becoming not so dead. I was pretty sure that there was some sort of word for that, but I could not for the life of me (quite an ironic saying coming from me) remember what it was. At first I did not notice, but after a while I tried to give him a treat and he was not at my feet where he usually had been.

Pulling on my cloak, and ventured out into the rain and saw the mangy wolf was laying with head on paws in the pouring rain looking out to where Grit had left from. Pity came over me, something I did not ever re-member feeling before, and it overwhelmed me.

I went to him and sat next to him. He put his head on my leg and whined.

"If she is not back by tomorrow, we'll go into the village and ask about her, okay?" This was not ideal. I did not know how the goblins would receive me com-ing into their main territory unannounced, but this did not seem true to Grit's nature. To just leave Grimmaw with me and not come back.

The wolf looked up at my wet, hooded, bony mug and licked it. "Great, more of your drool." I said and laughed, rubbing his head.

I rose to my feet and started walking back towards the hut. Half way I stopped and looked back at the wolf. "Grim, come!" I said and patted my side. The wolf looked up at me, then back towards where Grit had left. He sighed, rose, and came to my side.

The morning came, but Grit did not. Going into the goblin village was probably the second to last thing that I wanted to do that day. Sitting and watching the lake and maybe throwing a stick to Grimmaw would have been much better. Hells, counting blades of grass would have been better. The only thing worse would that I could think of would be going back to the skels. but I promised a wolf, and you really can not go back on a promise to a wolf. It just isn't done.

Grimmaw was waiting as I donned my cloak and hood, strapping my sword around my waist. I should have chosen my attire a bit more carefully.

I looked around Odem's hut, hoping it was not the last time I would be here. When I got next to the wolf, he bent down to me. At first I had no clue what he wanted, but after a moment or two, I mounted him. I guessed maybe he thought if I was riding him that maybe I would be accepted better with the goblins. Maybe he was used to it with Grit. I did not know.

Imagine seeing, maybe for the first time, a reanimated skeleton riding to the gates of your village on a warm morning. Now that would probably be scary, seeing how your people are currently in some sort of conflict with skeletons.

Now picture that this particular skeleton is dressed all in black, a cloak with a hood over his head (in my defense, I thought this would be more welcoming than riding bare-headed, my skull shining in the sun would be. I don't think that would have mattered much, truthfully) and a giant sword strapped to his hip.

If you have that picture in your mind, now put this black cloaked skeleton with a sword bigger than most of the people you know, and put him onto a giant wolf.

Not my best decision.

I had met or at least seen what seemed like hundreds of goblins from the village, so I thought that they would at least know who I was. There were two problems with this logic, though.

One, there were thousands of goblins in the village. Many more than I thought there would be.

And two, as I had said before, many of the goblins I had met did not like me.

We were not 'well met', as some would say.

Actually, we were 'well met' but with arrows and spears. I don't think they were trying to hit us though, or perhaps they just had horrible aim, as none of the projectiles came close to hitting us. But they definitely made their point.

Grimmaw made some horrible noises towards the gates, and the goblins made some horrible noises back. This was not an ideal situation. Tensions were high on both sides.

I decided to back Grimmaw up behind where the goblin projectiles could reach us. I was not very afraid for myself. Arrows had little effect on me, though they could do damage if I was hit just right. But, I did not want the wolf to get hurt by accident. I wanted to calm the whole situation down the best I could and find out what had happened to Grit. Then get out of there.

I unmounted the wolf, patted his neck and told him to "stay." I had no idea if he knew what I said or not, but he came when I said to, so I figure that it was worth a shot. I then found out that the goblins were just trying not to hit Grimmaw. With me, they had great aim.

I began to walk to the gate and the first arrow to 'hit' me went straight through my bones and my cloak, leaving a small tear. I sighed as best I could and looked at Grimmaw, who was now laying down moping. I pulled my sword to use as a shield and made my way through the rain of arrows.

Half way to the gate, I heard someone yell something. I did not quite understand it. It must have been in the goblin language that Grit and Zrakkon had been speaking on the double tackle day, but I got the gist of it.

The arrows stopped firing, and the gate opened.

I sheathed my sword as I saw Grit's grandfather coming out to greet me.

Chapter 7

Sorry That I Ruined Your Day

The conversation with Grit's grandfather was a bit on the boring side I must say. He's not much for words. I mean, he says a lot in a small amount of them. He seemed a bit perturbed that I was even there at first, to tell the truth.

Anyway, it went kind of like this:

I said, "Hello."

He said the same. Then he asked, "Why are you here?"

I said, "because Grit had left Grimmaw with me a few days ago and never came back. The wolf is a bit worried."

"The wolf?" He asked.

"Yes, seems a bit downtrodden and whatnot. We figured we'd check on her."

He kind of caught me off guard a bit with his reply, "The scout party never came back." It was straight to the point and cold. There was something in his eye, maybe a tear. I was not very good at reading people yet at that point. It may have been dust or something.

"Have you looked for them?"

"Oh yeah. They seem to have gotten trapped behind a human camp."

I was thinking this was a big deal, but he said it as if it wasn't. "Should we, maybe, go get them?"

"That's a good idea. Let me know how it goes." He said. Apparently, I had just volunteered to go get them.

"You want me to go?"

"Yes, you look scary. Maybe the humans will run away." With that, he turned to go back through the village gate.

"Umm, just one thing," I said after turning back towards the wolf, slightly flabbergasted.

He stopped and turned back to me. "Yes."

"I don't know where they went."

He laughed a bit. "Oh yeah, that would help, eh?"

"Yes, I think."

He pointed in a direction past the lake. "Over there and then to the north a bit."

And so Grimmaw and I left the goblin village and had a new mission, 'rescue the goblin scout squad.' I could tell right away that the wolf was on board.

One thing I learned that day is that giant wolves are not easy to sneak around.

Another is not to get directions from a goblin.

They are way too vague.

It would have been great if we could have gone up to the first person that we saw and said, "Have you, by chance, seen a small party of goblins come through here? It seems as though they have gotten themselves a bit lost." But, figuring that these goblins were spying on the humans that we were most likely to meet, this seemed to be a bad idea.

We did get to the other side of the lake with little difficulty. Which was when I realized that we probably should have waited until night to leave. Our side of the lake was very wooded and gave us great cover. The human side, though, not so much.

There were some rocky areas we could kind of slip in and out of, and of course, from a distance, I could pass as just a wandering human.

Grimmaw could not pass as anything but what he was, though, a giant wolf. At that time I did not know, but did suspect, that humans would be suspect of a giant wolf. Figuring that they were luring them away and killing them was my first hint.

Meeting some humans on the other side of the lake was my next.

"Hey there!" One said. I was trying to get us from one rocky hill to the next, really having no clue of where I was going, except north, when he surprised me.

I tried to keep my head low and under my hood, and pushed Grimmaw back behind a boulder. "Hey." I said back and gave a weird sort of wave to him.

There were three of them, altogether, two women and the male. They looked like they were on their way for a swim. I was hoping that the 'hey there' and my 'hey' back would be the end of the conversation and that they would be on their merry way, so I just stood there, waving too long.

I was wrong, of course. "What do you have there?" One of the women asked.

"Oh, nothing much, no," I said awkwardly. It came out much more suspicious than if I just started running away.

"Cattle?" the other woman asked.

"Oh no, no cattle here. Just a, um, human... me." I tried to save it. "Just a me." This was bad.

The man got in front of the women, why I wasn't sure as they both had already pulled daggers out, and look pretty frightening in the way that they stood. The man pulled a sword that I instinctively knew was way too big for him to wield properly. It probably made him feel good about himself, but he was more likely to hurt himself than anyone else.

"I don't want trouble, just looking for friends."

"Stealing cattle is more like it. Get him Josiah!" The first woman who had addressed me said. The other was egging him on as well.

This was not going to end well at all.

He rushed at me with the sword above his head, which took me off guard by how stupid it was. I was thinking about all the ways I could kill, maim, or just knock him over without even trying as he came.

In the end I just moved to the side as he tried to control his sword and stuck my foot out as he went by. He went flying and tried to twist towards me, saw Grimmaw and freaked out, slicing and breaking his own leg in the process. Nothing that would kill him if he got help, but he wouldn't be running any time soon. And he'd have a nasty scar.

Grimmaw moved towards him, but I raised my hand and said "stay." To my surprise, he stopped. I patted him for being such a good wolf.

The women, who at this time had started towards the Josiah fellow, stopped quickly. They did not yell or run away, but held their daggers defensively. I did admire them for that, although I guess it was kind of dumb to stand there staring at a giant wolf.

Grimmaw was growling with drool running down his maw. I held onto his mane, but I was pretty sure I was not going to be able to hold him back if he decided he wanted the women for lunch.

"I'd go if I were you. Believe me, the drool is pretty gross." I said.

I think that they caught a glimpse of my face as I tried to hold Grimmaw. Both of their faces froze up in a kind of freaked out look and turned quite pale. They dropped the daggers and ran.

Josiah was crying by this time. I didn't blame him much. His leg looked quite painful and his friends had just taken off. I imagined that they probably had a nice day planned, a little swimming, maybe a bit of frolicking.

"Sorry, I ruined your day." I said as I searched for a brace for the leg. "Do you think that they'll be back?"

"What?" He said. He seemed in a bit of shock. I figured me being a skeleton, and all, helped little in that regard.

"Will they come back? Or send someone for you?"

"I think so."

"Good. I don't think that your people would welcome me carrying you back."

He actually laughed at this. "No, probably not."

"You should get a smaller sword." I said as I brought two straight pieces of wood and put his leg between them. He grimaced, but surprisingly did not cry out. I flinched just looking at it.

"Why?"

"It's too big for you. You can't keep balanced." I said and looked for something to tie them together. I was acting on instinct, not really knowing what I was doing, but doing it anyway. I just hoped that I was not doing more damage. "Also, never charge like that again. I killed you about six ways in my mind."

"I think I'm hallucinating."

"Why?"

"It seems like a skeleton with a giant wolf is binding my leg and giving me sword fighting advice."

"Sadly, you're not." I said and started tying his leg with some rope they had brought along.

"Why are you helping me?"

"I don't know." I said, being honest. I saw him hurt and just started helping. It was automatic. "How far are they going?"

"I can't tell you that."

"Do I have time to sit a minute? Get some water for him." I nodded my head towards Grimmaw.

"You have some time. At least an hour, if anyone believes them right away." He thought a moment, "probably more."

"No one will believe them?"

"Not at first. I tend to do this. At night, maybe, when I don't come back." He looked deep in thought, so I gave the wolf some water.

"Why are you out here?" He asked.

"I told you, looking for a friend."

"Goblin?"

"The wolf give me away?"

He laughed and held his middle and forefinger close. "There is talk of some goblins trapped in a cave a few miles north."

"Why are you helping me?"

"Not sure, returning the favor, maybe." He was sweating now. Hopefully, they would come sooner than he thought. "My friend is there, though. Try not to hurt anyone."

"I will try. I hope someone comes soon for you."

He fidgeted a while. I could tell he was in a lot of pain, but he was trying not to show it. "Don't trust the goblins, they're evil."

"Maybe." I said and paused. "But they may say the same about you, you know?"

He thought about it, almost spoke, then stopped himself. He only said, "Maybe."

I looked at him. The sweat poured from him now. I hoped his people knew how to help. "Besides, did you think that a skeleton would be binding your leg today?"

He just looked down. Grimmaw and I left him there to be saved or to die. It was out of our control now. I did know that we needed to hurry a bit. Someone would be coming, and even if Josiah did not tell them where he sent us, the women would have mentioned the wolf.

Whoever came would figure out where we were going quite quickly.

I Thought That I'd Be the Hero

The wolf and I made our way towards where Josiah said that Grit may be. I did intend to keep my word to try to not hurt anyone. But if it came to it, I probably would have to. I worried a bit about the boy. In the end, he seemed nice, even if he had tried to impress some girls by attempting to destroy me.

I was pretty sure he was going to die, though. Not much to do about that now, except try to keep all the dying to a minimum.

I heard the humans talking way before I saw them. If a raiding party had come, they would have been slaughtered. I thought about just riding in there and trying to scare them off, but it sounded like a lot of people.

It may work for a few minutes, but not long.

We made our way around the hill and took refuge behind it. Grimmaw really wanted to go kill some humans and get to Grit, but I reasoned with him. Or, at least, I pretended to. I was not sure how much actually was getting through figuring he was, you know, a wolf. But in the end, he seemed to agree with me for the time being.

Then we waited. I figured that we would continue to until about sunset. Grit's grandfather said that I would be scary to them. Maybe we could use that to our advantage. Sunset seemed like the scariest time to show up.

I do have to say that we must have looked terrifically terrifying when the humans first saw us! This I know because there were about a dozen of them sitting outside of a cave, which, if I were a goblin hiding from humans, would be where I would go, and the humans ran away when they saw me.

I attribute this to two things, one I knew then and the other I found out later. The first was that it was the perfect sunset to come across their camp. The sky behind me was blood red, fading into a dark purple over them. This highlighted my visage quite well and brought the scary factor up.

The second was that humans have quite a few stories about a skeletal figure in a black cloak, and none of them are of the friendly sort. One is of a fellow who comes to reap you when you die. Strange that they equate themselves to crops, but oh well, it worked out.

Another foretells doom or death or some other bad omen. Now that one rides a horse, not a wolf, but they panicked real good, so either way.

There are a few others, I guess, but whatever they thought, they hightailed it out of there. I thought to myself that humans would be pretty easy to deal with in the future, but that turned out to be wrong. Once they see something, they get braver each time; it seems.

I made my way to the cave entrance and yelled, "Grit!" To you know, see if Grit was there.

Zrakkon was the first to come out, huffed at seeing me there, and said, "About time."

Three others came out, but not Grit. Two thanked me and the other was about as nice as the Zrakkon. He kind of just grunted something unintelligible. It could have been goblin speech, maybe. I'm pretty sure he just did not want me to hear it, though. Truthfully, I just didn't care at all. My intention was to find Grit and make the wolf happy. He seemed so miserable without her.

Then Grimmaw got excited, and I had to get off of him to not fall. Grit was coming, a bad cut on her arm, but nothing that would not heal. She seemed well. Happy even. Her smile radiated through the dim weather. Maybe I wanted to save her more than just for the wolf. Although, I did not want to admit that yet.

The vicious wolf ran to her and began licking her face, then licked her wound. Grit grimaced and patted her friend's head. She looked at me. "Thank you for taking care of him."

I nodded to her. "Of course."

The reunion was fun, but we had to go. I could already hear the humans coming back.

After the rescue of the scouting party, things seemed to go pretty well. Except, oddly enough, with Zrakkon.

Now, I say oddly enough, but you must remember that I was still in my newly not so dead naïve phase. I did not quite understand the whole bravado thing. You stole my glory; you made me look bad by saving me thing that was going on.

I saw him one day and went right up to him, trying to smile with no lips and waving. I was saying something like "Hey Zrakkon, buddy, how ya doing?" and what not.

He just leaned his shoulder into me and kept on walking, laughing with his buddies.

I would have thought maybe he didn't see me, but I stood out quite a bit. I just looked after him and his crew, with my mouth hanging open. Something, or someone rather, tugged on my cloak sleeve to pull me out of this dismay.

"Don't worry about him." It said (I hadn't quite looked down to see that it was a young boy goblin at this time,) "He's kind of mean."

"Oh." I replied, looking down at him.

"I'm Roji. Nice to meet you." He held out his hand to do their wrist grab greeting. I had not been doing this much, since they would have to grab the bone in my arm. I had only done it with Grit, who was teaching me in case of situations like this, and her grandfather, who insisted when I returned with the scout group.

I looked at Roji, then at my arm, then back at Roji. Grit had said that it was a great disrespect if you refused the greeting. I did not want that. But, I also didn't want to scare the child.

The boy took the decision away from me and grabbed my wrist, turning it back and forth, as was custom. "I am Bonesy." I said.

"I know." He felt my arm, and it was a strange sensation. I mean, I didn't actually feel it, but inside. This was only the fourth or fifth living thing to actually touch me, and he show no fear, no disgust at all. The other two don't really count either. Grit I was trying to kill the first time, Grimmaw was stopping me from doing so, and the grandfather felt he had no choice. And I guess the human, although I was setting his leg.

"Weird." He said of my arm. "Is that what's in my arm, too?"

"I imagine, yes. But smaller."

He started poking at his own arm, trying to feel the bone. "We're pretty much the same then, right?"

My face tried to smile. "I guess so, yeah."

"Roji. Roji, time to go." They heard his mother yell.

"I'll be back," the young goblin said as he ran off waving. "See you later."

"Later." I said and waved. By the look on his mother's face, I did not think that I would see him again.

But I did. And a lot. Just about every day.

Sometimes it was just for a quick "Hi." and then he'd run off to play with friends. Other times he would ask me questions about myself, which I had to usually say, "I don't know."

On one occasion, he came by when I was playing what Grit and I ended up calling 'Get the Stick' with Grimmaw. I had absolutely mastered my throwing technique by then and could throw it wherever I wanted.

Anyway, he came by and asked me where I came from. I tried to give him the same old story about being reanimated in the mountains, but he stopped me. "No, no. Not now, before."

"Before what?"

"Before this," He said, pointing to my bones.

"I don't remember."

"Hmm. You sure? I mean, shouldn't it be around here? If you died around here?"

"I hadn't thought of that." I lied. I thought about it a lot. "I may have traveled here, though."

"Maybe." He said and was off again.

This time, however, his mother came over to me.

I threw the stick, and Grimmaw ran after it. "Fine morning." I said.

"Yes, yes." She said.

"What can I do for you?"

She kept her head low, then said softly, "Stay away from my son."

"Roji?" I said. I was confused. "He always comes to me."

She looked me in the eye sockets. "You're always here. Stay away from him." She was more confident now.

"Why?"

Her head went down again. "I don't trust you." She looked behind her, quickly and towards the village. Zrakkon was standing with his crew. "No one does."

Chapter 8

It's Jeff

There were many more interactions such as this, but this is the one that has stood out to me. Every day that I stayed there after that day, and that woman's words, the boy would come. He would look at me, and instead of what was once curiosity and friendship, there was fear.

I can only imagine what the boy's mother had told him, but his face told me it was horrible. Many other children had a similar look or just stopped coming.

I was an outcast again, in what I had thought could have been my home. Even Grit and Grimmaw came only once to visit that week. They were quite friendly visits, but I could tell that Grit was looking over her shoulder to see who was watching us.

The final straw, as they say, came in the middle of the night. I was lying in my (or really Odem's) bed, trying to pretend that I could sleep when I heard them. For a group that knew that I did not sleep, they were either stupid, or not afraid, for they were not stealthy at all.

Unfortunately, I feel the latter is the case.

They came in the middle of the night and lit the hut on fire. It went up so quick that there really was no time for me to put it out. I went to grab my stuff, but realized quickly that I did not have much, just my sword, really.

I did go back in for my journals. Or, to be truthful, some of Odem's journals that I had been using. And a bag. A bound leather satchel that I could only believe was Odem's pack at some point. I threw this journal and a few more in, along with my writing utensils, and I left for the woods.

I heard Zrakkon and his posse laughing and yelling, "Where ya gonna stay now, Bonesy?" and other things that I wish not to repeat. It took a lot not to just go kill them, but I resisted.

Thinking, for a moment, that I could go to the village and talk with Grit and maybe her grandfather, but it seemed useless.

It was time to go.

But where?

I sat for a bit as the hut burned, and Zrakkon taunted me. The skels were out of the question, and so were the humans. Even if I wanted to go there, they would not have accepted me, anyway. And if Josiah and his girls had spoken bad about me, well, that would not work out at all.

Figuring the goblins lay south, the humans east and the skels, who I really did not want to go back to, were west, that left north.

So north I went.

It really would have been better traveling with someone else, although of the people I had met since being reanimated, I could only see myself traveling with Grit and Grimmaw, and he wasn't even humanoid. Maybe Odem he wasn't so bad, but at the moment, he was dead.

Everyone else pretty much sucked. Well, Grit's grandfather wasn't half bad, but I would not think that he would be a splendid travelling companion.

Anyway, there really weren't many options. And of the few options, none of them were coming with me anyway, so I set out on my own. Maybe I could run into some people more like Odem. I think, though, that part of his charm was that he could not see me for what I was. That may be too harsh on a guy who treated me well, but everyone who had seen me seemed to want me dead again.

I thought for a bit that maybe I should head back towards the skels. Maybe track down Jeff (I still did not know his name then, so I still called him Jeff) and see if he could explain why I was sentient and the rest of the skels were not. I shook this thought after a while though, figuring that trusting someone who reanimated corpses to fight in an army was probably not the way to go.

Besides, who would I ask? It is not like any of them ever responded to me. I could not just go into the skel camp and ask someone, 'hey, where's Jeff?' They would probably just hand me yet another sword and make me attack someone.

No, it was most likely best just to try my luck somewhere else.

Too bad that I did not know anywhere else. That would have been a great help. So north I went.

I left Zrakkon and his laughing minions behind and rambled on towards the mountains. The journey was not very difficult, pretty much flat lands and woods, but then again, I did not make it very far.

Not very far at all.

Like I said, the travel was pretty easy, especially for someone who does not get tired. Or have to eat. Or go to the bathroom. Or really do anything at all. I just walked.

I could tell that it was getting cold, the weather was changing. Winter was coming. I could feel that, but not that it was cold. Cold was a thing I would never feel again, seemingly, no matter how long I 'lived.'

It was weird that you would miss cold.

Not that I did then. That took a long time to miss, to tell the truth. Mainly, of course, due to the fact that at that time, I did not remember what cold was.

I remembered later.

This night, I just walked. I walked for a while northward, trying to get at least to where I could pass the humans without being seen. It was hard to judge. I moved north, then a bit east, then north some, then east. Then I smelt it. The smell of firewood in the air. I stayed hid, but crept closer. I was not exactly sure why. The smart thing to do was to go away from the smell of firewood.

Then I heard them.

Humans.

They seemed to be minding their own business, and except for looking a bit military-esque, they seemed quite harmless. I waited for a while to see if they would eventually leave, but they appeared to be waiting for something.

There were twelve of the humans that I could see, but I remembered my first meeting with Grit's grandfather and looked to the trees.

Sure enough, two more were hidden with bows.

Something was happening. I just did not know what. I decided, at this point, to lie low and wait it out. There really was not much else to do. I had nowhere to be, and I did not know if there may be more in the trees that I did not see. No need to draw attention to myself for no reason.

A few hours in, I was getting bored with what was going on; I had thought a few times that I should just leave, contemplating where to go, figured there was not a way to go that was satisfying and decided to stay, when a human came out of the trees with skels in tow.

From his attire, it looked like Jeff and, if I was not mistaken, the skel whose foot I inadvertently knocked off.

Seemed that he was doing pretty well for himself, if it was, in fact, him. Hanging out with the man himself. I was kind of happy that he was there and doing well. I mean, I was not one-hundred percent sure that he was the same skel, but how many would be running around with only one foot.

Maybe a few, actually, I thought. It felt better to just believe that it was him, though, so I decided to.

The humans and Jeff did not seem to openly like each other, but no one was trying to kill or destroy anyone else, so I figured this was the meeting that the humans were waiting so long for. They seemed to be a little bit peeved about the lateness, but I could not hear much.

Moving myself over towards the skel side, I shimmied on my stomach, or what used to be my stomach, to get far enough up to hear what was being said. I was close and could catch a few words. One of which was absolutely 'goblins.' This piqued my interest. Even though they shunned me, they did take me in for a while. I did not really want anything bad to happen to them.

Well, maybe Zrakkon.

And Zrakkon's posse.

I thought about this and decided that even though I was not a big fan of them, and in the end probably would not care either way if they died, if they were attacked, it would not bode well for the other goblins.

So I shimmied some more and tried to get into a better position to hear what was going on.

That is where my mistake happened.

I desperately tried to keep myself from sliding down the hill.

I failed.

I not only slid down the slope, but in my attempt to grab onto anything that may keep me from sliding down the hill, I managed to begin rolling down the hill.

The humans pulled their weapons. The skels pulled their own.

Luckily, in this minor scuffle and with the addition of the darkness, no one really seemed to notice me file in with the other skels. I pulled my sword and stood the line with the others.

"Sheath your weapons." Jeff commanded, and the skels obliged.

I also felt compelled to put my sword away, but this time, it seemed more like a strong suggestion than a command. I did and stood in the back of the others, trying to hide myself.

"Put them away." A human said. He was much younger than Jeff, but very much in command of the human side.

Jeff's gaze seemed to linger in my direction, and I thought that I saw a faint smile form, but then dismissed it as my imagination. I did not fit in with the others, seeing how I had a cloak on and my sword was not the standard issue, but it was dark. I would have to sneak away if the opportunity presented itself.

The boss human and Jeff had some words with each other, each blaming the other for the commotion.

The human mentioned how Jeff seemed to have another abomination. I took a little offense to this, thought about it, and kind of agreed to the term.

Jeff mentioned the archers in the trees.

In the end, they agreed to just get their meeting started and over with so they could all just go home.

"Is the queen on board?" Jeff asked. From my new vantage point, I could hear much better. My training paid off well, figuring that I knew the skels would not move unless ordered. It helps to stand perfectly still when you do not get tired or need to breathe.

The humans were not as still and kept moving about. This did not seem to faze Jeff, though.

"She's not a queen... ah, never mind," the boss human began, "The mayor will be. She wants the goblins gone as much as we all do."

"I doubt that." Jeff said. "We will attack from the west in a week's time. I trust you will be ready to do the same from the east."

The human looked confused. "The plan has not changed?"

"It has not."

"We will be ready at the scheduled time then," the human boss said. "Once they are exterminated, the truce will end."

"I would not have it any other way," the necromancer said, and he got up to leave. "Tell your queen she has my word."

"She is not..." The human started, then turned to his people, "What is it with this guy? Let's go."

"Come." was all Jeff said, and the skels turned with him. I was compelled to go, but still not as strongly as before I left them. The draw was stronger than when I first fell down the hill, though. I had to get away.

When Jeff passed by me, his head turned. I thought, for a quick moment, that he was going to stop and address me. I thought that I had been caught, but he gave that slight grin and kept moving.

I would have let out my breath if I had been holding it, but I can't hold my breath, so I couldn't let out my breath.

I had two very related problems at that moment. I needed to get away from the skels, and Jeff, without being seen, and I needed to warn the goblins, or at least Grit, of their impending doom.

Chapter 9

What's With My Arm

You would think that escaping from a dozen skeletons that seem unaware that you are even there
would not be much of a problem. You, as I was, would
be wrong. Although, I think that the bigger problem
was Jeff.

Not that he was really paying much attention that I
could tell. He seemed not the most trusting sort, however, and sent two of the skels to watch our back.

"Destroy anything that may come between you and
us." He said. And this was the kick. I could have been
hallucinating a bit, or just paranoid, but I was pretty
sure that he gave me just the subtlest of looks. I tell
you this though, it was not lost on me that he may be
pretty sure that I did not belong. Hells, if I were Jeff, I
would be quite suspicious.

I wanted to say something, but could not think of
anything that may be relevant at that particular time.

'The goblins aren't all bad,' came to mind, but I dismissed it.

'Do I know you from somewhere?' Also popped into my skull, but I passed.

"Come!" he said. This time, I felt my legs begin to move without my will. I definitely had to get out of there before Jeff's influence took total control.

Now, I was a bit stuck, though.

I lost track of where the skels had gone behind us. Jeff most definitely knew that I did not belong, and for all I knew, the humans were following and waiting for the opportunity to ambush the whole lot of us.

All I wanted to do was get Grit and Grimmaw away from the village, and I seemed to only have about a week to do that.

Maybe that little boy and the grandfather too, I was not very sure at that point.

The main priority was to escape my current situation, and that seemed as if it may be a bit of a difficult venture. You would think that I could just run away.

You know, round a corner or something and make a break for it.

This would be a sound plan, if I was a running sort. You see, I may be able to walk for, well, maybe eternity. I never really felt tired at all, but my running speed was not that spectacular. I tried it a few times, not very fast at all.

Kind of slow, actually.

I tried planning out a real plan. Maybe take out the skels one by one, hoping that Jeff would not notice, then run once the numbers were low. I did not think that I would have much trouble taking them out, except for the whole 'if I don't destroy them they just keep moving' thing.

Besides, I did not know if the whole telepathic thing worked both ways and that Jeff would know if I attacked.

In the end, though, we rounded a corner, and I decided, well maybe instinct took over because I did not think about it much, to make a break for it. I saw a slight break in the trees and I just ran.

I did not at any time look back. I had no clue, really, if anyone was following me. I just ran as fast as I could.

I seemed to hear Jeff's voice in my head say 'don't go, come back' but it sounded extremely sarcastic and I was not quite sure if it was actually him or just in my head. Either way, I did not listen.

I just kept running.

It was not long before I knew the skels were following. At least some of them.

I could feel them getting close. I am not sure why it was that they ran faster than me; I guess that it was the doing of Jeff, but I could not be sure. But man, they were fast.

I realized quickly that running was not the answer. I had to fight. And the fight had to be quick.

Jeff's thoughts were burrowing into my brain, or whatever the Hells I had for one, and I could tell that I would not be able to resist him for long. "Come back," it said to me. "Come home." The word 'home' did have a good feel to it, I would have had to admit.

I was quite sure, however, that this was a trick though. Something to get me to stay a wee bit too long and let Jeff exert his telepathic control.

The skels were close now.They were not as quick as I was, though, as I turned on the first one to reach me and slashed him through. He crumpled in half and fell by my feet, reaching out to grab me.

I kicked his hand away. "One down." I looked to see three others in pursuit. I was hoping these were the only four that Jeff spared to chase me down. At least they were not staying together. Two were about the same speed. The last, who I did not want to face, was limping on one foot.

I turned and ran further, trying to get some separation between the three.

"Come HOME!" Jeff's voice demanded.

"Never," I thought.

"But we are your family." The voice said. I staggered at this and because of a branch that caught my foot.

"You can hear me?" I asked. This felt both astonishing and a complete and utter breach of my privacy. Me hearing him seemed odd, but okay, he was trying to let me hear him, but this?

"Yes. Come home," he said.

"Get out of my head." I said as the next skel reached me. I misjudge this completely, although I think I can be at least a little bit excused by my distraction.

He struck my left arm. Quite hard too. So hard that it detached from my shoulder.

It did not break though.

It also did not fall as it should have.

As I spun around to face my attacker, my arm still followed my will. It flew around me and struck the offending skel in the face with such a force that it took its head off.

"That's new," I said and raised my sword to fend off its last real attack, having already started swinging at me. The sword fell from its hand and the skel dropped to the forest floor. Crawling around, trying desperately to find its head.

His partner was there immediately, so I had no time to see if he ever found it.

This one was pretty skilled with his sword and I, being one arm down, had some trouble keeping pace.

As we parried each other's swords time and time again, I saw the limping skel coming.

"They will destroy you," Jeff said.

"Not today."

"What is with your arm?" Jeff asked.

"What do you mean?" I thought-asked him.

"It seems to be... I don't know... detached." I felt I had an upper hand here, pun I guess intended. He knew something was off, but at least he could not see through my eyes. At least not yet.

"Nothing, it's fine." I thought-told him. I felt lying was probably the best course of action just then. Although, in truth, I was not exactly sure it was lying. The arm seemed perfectly fine, hovering at shoulder level, just waiting for me. Either way, Jeff did not need to know that I could control and reattach my severed limbs.

Jeff did, inadvertently, help me out by reminding me that I could use my left arm. It took a moment to get used to as my first attempt sent it flying off into the woods.

By the time I got it to come back, we had moved some, and it flew right between us and off to the other side of the woods. This happened a few more times.

Trying to defend with my right arm and learn to control my flying left proved challenging, but eventually I got it to come back to me. I waved it in front of the skel's face to make sure that I did have control and then had it grab its sword arm.

This gave me enough of an opening to render him harmless, for the time being.

"Destroy!" Jeff thought said into my head.

"Not today," I thought replied.

"Come home." it was sad, he was feeling desperate at this point.

"No." I replied, fleeing as the footless skel was getting close.

Chapter 10

Oh, How I Would Love A Pickle and Other Ponderings

As I was running straight on towards the goblin village, a few things popped into my thoughts:

The first was that it was quite humorous that my arm was doing a running motion while floating in the air next to where it should have been attached to my body. I kept looking at it in absolute wonder.

The second was that the footless skel was not going to stop. He would follow me to the village and would not be very welcome.

A third thing was that Jeff was now not popping into my thoughts.

I was not sure what to think of this third thing. Did he just give up, or had I put enough distance between us to break the connection? I was not sure which one I was hoping for.

Either way, I had to do something about one-foot guy. If he made it to the goblin village, the goblins would destroy him. They may also think that I had something to do with him coming there. Neither of those things was what I wanted to happen.

I also did not want to engage him. I already knocked off his foot, and even though he seems to have done well for himself since then, I still felt a little guilt in that.

I was, as they say, in a pickle.

Although I am not entirely sure why they say this, or who 'they' actually are. All I knew at that moment was that I needed a way to not destroy one-foot guy or lead him to the goblins. I also needed, somehow, to get to the goblins and warn them about this impending attack.

And now I wanted, more than anything else, to taste a pickle. Hells, I did not even know what a pickle tasted like anymore. This, oddly enough, made me extremely sad. Just that most likely I would never, ever taste one again.

I decided that it would be best to take a tangent off the trail and away from the goblins for the moment. Turning right, which seemed a good idea, figuring if the two skels Jeff had sent behind the group would be to the left of us, and found a nice boulder to sit on and contemplate my situation.

I sat upon the large rock and grabbed my left arm, holding it to where it was once attached, then unattached, then reattached and now unattached again. I was hoping for it to reattach.

It took a lot longer than the last time and for a bit I was in a state of panic. I tried pulling it away and placing it ever so slowly where it was supposed to be. I tried jamming it into my shoulder. Once, I even tried to reason with it a little, telling it to attach to its home. Eventually, when I was about to give up, I let it go and it just stayed where it was supposed to.

I want to say that it tickled a bit when reattaching. Maybe not, but I definitely felt a sensation I had not felt since being recently not-so-dead. Maybe, I was starting to get back my sense of feeling. Maybe I, someday, could taste a pickle. Maybe, it was just because it was off for so long.

Either way, I was concerned about it.

Was it because it flew so far away from me? Did I take too long to reattach it? Was it damaged from the blow? I certainly did not want to end up as a bunch of unattached limbs trying to keep track of where everything was.

And why were Jeff's commands not working? Had I been away too long? I did sense that it was getting harder to resist him the longer I stayed near him. If I was there longer, would he had taken control back?

I spent way too much time thinking about this and did not notice that one-foot guy had caught up to me and was currently trying to climb the boulder.

He was not very good at it and kept sliding back down. It seemed that I had a little more time to think about these problems.

I watched as one-foot guy tried and tried to climb the boulder and get to me. Although I had seen him use a bow and sword, and I was sure that he probably only got better with practice, he was no climber. I felt comfortable that I had plenty of time to ponder.

So, ponder I did.

One-foot guy was looking up at me as I pondered, so I figured 'what the Hells' and told him a bit about what the goblins had done. I started back at meeting Grit, reminding him that he was there for a part of it.

I ended with the burning of the hut. He seemed quite indifferent about the whole thing, but he was, at that moment, the only other thing there, so I kept on. "And so, if I had not run into you all and your little plot, I would be long gone by now." I said to him. He looked curious for more. Not really, but I pretended.

"I could still just leave and you and your skel friends would..." I stopped and looked at him, "well, probably not you actually. You would most likely just follow me. I'm afraid you are somewhat like me, a little abandoned for the time being."

He looked rather sad at that comment. Maybe it was just in my head. He did finally find some catch and began to pull himself up onto the boulder, though. I pushed his hand with my foot and he slid back down, starting again.

"See, this is my problem, that you are not going away." I rubbed my shoulder where it had reattached. Not really for any reason, it just felt instinctual.

"I can leave and you would follow. Maybe if I got far enough away, Jeff's influence could wane, but how far and how long will that take?" I played with the hilt of my sword, "If it would even work at all."

"I could just abandon the goblins. They would probably be fine, don't you think?" I asked. One-foot guy did not think so, though. I could tell.

"Most of them would deserve it, anyway." This was more to me than him, but he did start pulling himself up the boulder again. I kicked him down once more. "Well, some."

I paused and pondered, "Maybe not Grit or Grimmaw. Or the other wolves. Or the children. They were just mimicking their parents." I thought about a bunch of others who did not deserve it. It was a long list. Pretty much everyone except Zrakkon and his crew.

"You know what, One-foot? I did not need them to accept me completely. Just as they did Odem." I said, wanting to sigh, "I could have been happy, I think, living in the field and watching the wolves. You know I even came up with a name: 'Bonesy's Wolf Watching Service.'"

To me, one-foot guy looked impressed, "Obviously I would not have charged them. Besides, what do we need money for, anyway?"

That was when I heard the others coming. Half of one skel crawling his way and another running towards us. "You called your friends? I thought that we had something going on here."

His face changed, or rather, had never been what I had seen, to just a skel, with no emotion or any hint of understanding. Is that what I look like?

Probably.

The thing with skels was their numbers. Without that advantage, they were not much to deal with. I slid down the boulder and unsheathed my sword. With one motion, I removed my sword and took his head from his neck. The only skel that was not coming now was headless, so I figured that may be the key.

One-foot guy still tried to get me, pulling himself and reaching out, but he could not find me now.

I took out the other crawler in a similar manner. The runner was a bit more trouble, but not much. I left the boulder and continued to the goblin village. If nothing else, I could try to warn them.

Looking back at the skels crawling around, attacking each other and looking for their heads that they may never find, I felt pity for them.

They did not ask for this.

I just hoped that they were not like me. That they were mindless and did not know what had become of them.

Chapter 11

A Warm Welcome Back at the Goblin Village

After stashing the skulls in a quite hard to reach place, I made my way to the goblin village. It was cruel, I know, but in the long run, it was much better than destroying the skels outright. Especially since I had no idea about what their ultimate fate, or mine for that matter, would be.

Besides, I thought, they would find them eventually. Maybe not the correct ones, but well, they were probably interchangeable.

The village was not very far from my confrontation with the skels. It was but a hop, skip, and a jump away. Not that I was doing any of those silly things per se, I would look ridiculous if I had done so.

I did try a bit of a skip to be perfectly honest, but it felt off, so I stopped.

I went the roundabout way to the village, cursing myself for doing so, but I felt it was prudent given my having been followed earlier and the fact that Jeff could get all up in my brain sometimes. The wasted time probably mattered little though, as the goblins were happy to welcome me with shooting arrows and rocks in my general direction when I got to the village walls.

This went on for quite some time, too long, if you asked me. I am sure that they may have been having a joke in my direction by the end of things.

Eventually, I heard a yell in the goblin tongue that I could only equate to someone yelling 'cut it out there' since the goblins did indeed cut it out and stopped throwing things at me.

The gates opened and out came Grit, Grimmaw, the grandfather, and, to my dismay, Zrakkon.

Zrakkon was probably the last goblin that I wanted to see at that point. To be honest, I probably wasn't the first skel that he wanted to see either. So in that respect, I guess we were even.

"Well met!" I shouted, although it certainly seemed that we were not, with all the arrows and rocks and whatnot that had been thrown at me. Grit ran to me, as did Grimmaw, and gave a great hug. Well, not Grimmaw. He just licked my face, but Grit almost tackled me. I thought that I might lose my arm again.

"I thought that you were gone forever." The girl goblin said.

"Me too," Zrakkon added.

"Me too," I decided to add while waving to the grandfather with my, thankfully still attached, arm.

To my delight, he waved back and even had a bit of a smile on his face.

Zrakkon pulled his sword. "The question, of course, is why are you back?" he said.

"Not for a good reason, I am afraid." I said, "But it is great to see you two." I patted Grit and Grimmaw on the head, simultaneously.

Zrakkon said something to his grandfather in goblinese, but the older man shushed him. "Let him speak." The grandfather said, "And let us speak in a language he understands for the moment."

I appreciated that. It is a weird feeling when people speak in another language in front of you when you know that they speak a language that you do understand. Sometimes, it is fine if they are clarifying things or interpreting, but whatever Zrakkon said, I am sure that it was not nice. Either way, we continued.

"The skels and humans are coming for you." I said.

Zrakkon got immediately in my face and said some things I am quite sure, that if they were in a language I understood, would have implicated me as a spy or something. Grit tried to pull him off me. Grimmaw did.

After all that settled down, the old goblin turned and hobbled his way through the village gates. Grit pulled on the cloak that she had given me, and I followed her in. Zrakkon followed behind.

I could feel his eyes burning into me as we headed to what I guessed was the grandfather's house.

He went about as if he was just having the kids over for a visit, and not as if his village was going to be attacked. He told Grit and her cousin to sit and relax while he made something that resembled the coffee that Odem drank. The smell was different, though. Kind of fruity.

It was then I that I wondered why it was that I could smell, and hear and see for that matter, but not taste or feel. That thought gave me a shimmer of hope that I may some day; although that quickly deteriorated into thinking that I may lose my senses that I had as well. This led to me unconsciously poking my arm until I saw Grit shrug at me in a 'what the hells are you doing?' sort of way, so I stopped.Zrakkon kept tapping his hands on his wooden seat and hemming to say something between gazes at me. When he got too fidgety, the old goblin would give him a look, and he'd stop. But he'd start again quickly. The tapping getting faster each time. The old man asked Grit about her day and how everything was going. It was like any normal day; it seemed.

After Grit gave her account of the day, the grandfather turned to Zrakkon. By now, the veins in the cousin's forehead, which were quite bulging in normal circumstances, were absolutely throbbing. I was pretty sure that if I wanted to, I could have figured out his pulse from across the room. For the moment, at least, the rage was not towards me, though.

"And you, Zrakkon?" Grit stifled what I assumed was a giggle.

Zrakkon, to his credit, took a deep breath and paused. "I think that we should learn what this skeleton knows and figure out a plan."

"Yes, you are probably right. I do think that it is important to remember why we must fight though, don't you?" he turned to me and took me by surprise.

I, in my eternal wisdom of being not so dead for I didn't know how long, and caught by surprise by the question, said something that made little sense in the context of the conversation. Later, when I was leaving, I thought up a pretty good line about making sure that we make time for family and what-not.

I was quite upset with myself both times.

"Well, yes then, I suppose," the grandfather said to my odd reply. "I guess you're right, Zrakkon. What do you know?"

Everyone turned to me as I realized that I pretty much already told them everything I knew, so I said it again. Humans, skels, a week. That's about it. They seemed disappointed. I tried to add something, but nothing really came out.

Even Grit looked a bit disappointed with me, but it may have been my own disappointment in myself projected onto her.

"Well then, we must get the..." the grandfather started, but Zrakkon interrupted.

"Not in front of him." He said. To this, I was a bit hurt.

"He is not the enemy, cousin." Grit said.

Zrakkon stood his ground, "Even if he isn't, and I am not sure about that, he has even said that this Jeff has been in his head." He looked at me. I had to acknowledge that he was right with a nod. "Who says he's not still there?"

They looked at me again. "I don't feel him there." I finally said.

"Can you be sure?" Grit asked.

I couldn't. I really couldn't be sure if Jeff was there or not. It wasn't like there was some alarm that told me he was. Sometimes he just started talking in my head.

"I'm sorry." Grit said, but she did not need to be. I could not be responsible for the skels knowing whatever the goblins were going to do.

I said goodbye to my only friend and left for the second time.

Chapter 12

Razing

I was devastated, being thought of as a spy, even as an unwilling one. It was also quite unnerving to think that Jeff may still be in my head without me even knowing it. It's like that feeling you get when you're by yourself in a house and you just think someone or something else is there. You know no one is, but that doesn't really help at all.

But I also did not know that no one else was there. It was freaky.

It did not matter much now either way, though. I was on my own again. I passed by what was Odem's house on the way out, feeling what seemed to be sadness. Not really about what was, but what could have been.

Shaking it off, I kept moving. I did not get very far. Again.

The night had come, and I heard voices from over a hill. I was a bit bored, so I figured that I might check it out.

It was that kid and the two girls again. The one with the broken leg and the too big for him sword. I could not quite remember his name, which having broken his leg, I was embarrassed about. I watched the three of them for a while and then felt that was a little creepy, so I said "Hi."

I noticed right away that for one, the kid had a much smaller and more manageable sword, and two, although the girls jumped at my sudden appearance, none of them were as spooked by me as before.

They all, after righting themselves, said a version of "oh, hi," back to me.

It actually felt pretty good to be recognized and not made a big deal of for a change. The kid (I had resigned myself to wait and see if someone else would say his name so I would not insult him by not remembering) even offered me a drink. Which I, of course, declined since it would just spill on the ground and give me no enjoyment whatsoever.

To my surprise, they invited me to sit a spell and join them. I admit that it was awkward; I was not tired, and I really just wanted to keep going, but they were being rather nice about it and the laughter was inviting.

"What are you doing out here?" I asked. "I figured you were more lake people."

"Normally yes," said the boy whose name I could not remember. Joseph maybe. Jeremiah. Not quite right. Close, I had thought. But not quite. It was actually killing me inside enough to not really pay much attention to whatever it was he said next.

"Excuse me?" I said.

The brunette giggled at that.

"I did not hear you," I said.

"We are here to watch the attack," He repeated.

This took a moment to register. I do not think that I am slow in any way, but when faced with two contradictory ideas, my mind seemed to have a way of sort of pausing. "Attack on what?" I said.

The guy who I could not remember's name looked at me, as did the girls, in a way that made me feel way too stupid. "The goblin village." The blond one said.

"The goblins," I said in disbelief. They were coming too soon. As I have said, I was no good at keeping track of time, but it could not have been a week already.

"Yeah." The kid said in a tone that made me want to lop his head off. I may have, if the girls were not there, but that seemed a bit too, well, predictable for a skeleton.

"I thought…" I started, but could not finish.

I sat down on a fallen tree next to my three companions. My head sank into my hood and my hand fell to the hilt of my sword. A tickle formed in the darkest part of my nonexistent brain. It was there, though, the tickle. And it was growing. Growing into a giggle and then a laugh.

"Are you all right?" the blond asked.

"Not by a long shot," I replied to her and tried to wink to subside the look on her face. I realized I could not. I mean, if I had thought about it, I knew I could not for a long time, but the realization just came to me.

I had not blinked since becoming not quite dead. I could not shut off my sight as I used to unless I covered my eye sockets. I tried it to make sure I could. When I pulled my arm from my eyes, the three were looking at me with a look on their faces that gave me chills. Pity, I think it was.

I never wanted to see that look again.

I wished for a taste of what they were drinking. Longed for it, and I did not even know what it was. Anything to make the tickle, now giggle which would soon grow into laughter in my head go away.

I thought, at first, that the laughter in my head was mine. Maybe hoped was a better word.

But it was Jeff.

Had he been there the whole time? Even back before I saw him talking to the humans? The one human did appear confused about the 'week's time' comment. He had to have been there, or at the very least knew that I was around. And he let me go back to warn the goblins. Or go back with him. He really seemed to want me to. What the Hells did he want with me?

I sat with the three teens and watched as the battle began and ended rather quickly. They cheered a bit but were definitely subdued.

The boy looked on intensely, moving himself with every sound. With every slight glimpse we could get. He was like an injured player watching his team play without him. Rooting them on. But he knew that his companion was rooting for the other team.

To their credit, they tried to not openly cheer when the village went ablaze. The sparkle in the boy's eye told the truth, though. He wanted the goblins dead. And he wanted to be there killing them.

I know what you are thinking: why did I not do something? Why did I not run back and help? Or at the very least, warn them.

And I thought of doing just that, but I felt that it was fruitless.

Even if I had left as soon as I learned of the attack being today, I would not have made it in time. And even if I had, what then? From the sounds, there were hundreds of humans. More so of the skels. I seemed to be a trained fighter, but I was no match for those numbers. Maybe I would have killed a few humans, maybe destroyed a few skels. In the end, I would have been a pile of dust at the foot of the village gate. And the goblins fate would not have changed any.

We heard the humans leaving as the fires settled, and my companions decided that it was time to go. We hadn't spoken in quite some time and I just sat there staring at the flames of the burning village.

"I am sorry." The blonde said.

I looked up at her, ready to chastise her for the insincerity of her comment, but her eyes were low, barely looking at my own eye sockets. There was no fear there, as there was before. Tears were in her eyes.

"Thank you," was all I said. I wished that I had been better company and had at least asked her name, but it was what it was at this point. She touched my should for a brief second and turned to catch up with the others.

I watched her go for a moment and turned back to the fire with eyes that could not blink. Could not close. Just the reds and orange and yellow burning into my brain. And the dark, dark smoke.

And the laughter.

The horrible, unending laughter.

Chapter 13

Aftermath

The humans left long before the skels. It seemed that they were searching for something. Survivors maybe. I stayed my distance, not wanting to tip off to Jeff where I was. No, that's not true.

I was scared. I justified it in many ways to myself at the time. Looking back now, it was simple. I was terrified of what would happen to me if I got too close to Jeff again. I did not want to be a prisoner in my own body again.

So I waited. I waited until the flames subsided and I was sure, quite sure, that all the skels had left. Then I went to the village. There were no greetings of arrows and rocks. No yelling in a foreign tongue at me. Not even the walls survived. The razing was complete. If the skels had one specialty, it was complete destruction.

I knew why the skels stayed so long after the razing of the goblin village. They broke every building, every structure to dust. The food. The... It was too much.

I yelled for Grit, for Grimmaw, for the grandfather. There was no answer from anyone. Until a small noise, a knocking upon some wood. Distant, but there. I tracked it down through the rubble and heard it stronger. Grunting too.

"Help!" I barely heard as I yelled if anyone was there.

It was tiresome work as I pulled stones and wood from where the sound was coming. I guess tiresome is relative. I probably could have done it forever, but it was boring. As I got closer, I recognized the voice. For a moment, I wanted to stop and leave.

But I did not. I kept pulling. After pulling for what seemed like hours, Zrakkon was free. And not at all happy to see me.

"You!" He said, coming towards me. You would have never known that just a few seconds ago he had been buried under a ton of rubble. "You have a lot of nerve showing your face, or what's left of it, here!"

"Where's Grit?" That was all I could say.

With that, something else moved a ways away with a growl. I knew that growl and I went to pull the rubble away. Zrakkon even came to help. Together, we pulled Grimmaw out. He shook dust and debris from his fur and licked my face. If I had a face, it would have smiled. At least the wolf was safe.

"I don't know," Zrakkon said, sitting in the dirt.

"What?" I said.

"We evacuated the littles and the elders, besides my grandfather. He would not leave. Next would have been those who had the least experience fighting." He paused and drew a breath. "The youngers, the pregnant women. We had so little time."

He looked up at me with eyes I had not seen in him. Distraught, I would say. "You said a week's time."

I did not know what to say. "That is what I heard."

"Well, we had no time." He rose and dusted his hands. "Grit was taken, as were others. My grandfather."

"Where?" I asked.

He shrugged, "Who knows? The humans took some, the skels I think, took someone."

"Grit."

"How do you know?" He asked.

"He wants me. Jeff wants me." I said, more to myself than to him.

"And he took Grit..."

"To get to me." I interrupted. "It is the only leverage he has." I patted Grim and tried to give him an encouraging look. It failed.

"Then we must go to him," Zrakkon said.

"Not yet. We must rescue the others," I replied.

"My cousin."

"And my friend." I looked at him in the eyes. I did not know if it was soothing or not, but I needed him. "She will be fine. He wants me. We can use the time to get the others."

~

"So," Zrakkon said to me, "Your great idea is for you, a skeleton, and me, a goblin, to somehow sneak into the human village to rescue everyone there?"

"I see no other choice." I said. "Oh, and Grimmaw."

"So," He said again, "Your great idea is for a skeleton, a goblin, and a wolf to sneak into the human village to rescue everyone?"

"Well, we'd do it at night." I replied.

"Sounds like the start of a bad joke." He said, along with something else that I could not understand. I let it go as he looked over at what was left of his village. It was, after all, a horrible plan. We had no idea where they were, how many there were, or even if they were alive. All we really had was that Zrakkon heard what he thought was them being taken away.

"What I don't get is where are the bodies." He mumbled.

"Sorry?" I said, hoping that he would not repeat it.

"The bodies?" He said, to my regret louder and clearer. "I know that they took some prisoners, but there should be bodies. There are none."

I tried to look him in the eyes, but I could not and the words would not come to my mouth.

"The skeletons." He whispered.

He turned his gaze to me, his brow lowered more than it normally was, and his eyes narrowed to almost shut. I waited for the explosion to come. It never did. I hoped that it would, but after staring straight into my soul, or a reasonable facsimile of a soul, he just took a breath and walked by me.

"It will be night in a few hours. I am going to rest. Try not to get me killed as well." He bumped me as he went by. I did not blame him.

When the sun dropped itself over the horizon and the sky began to turn a dark purple, we left. He said nothing to me except that "It is time."

We got to the outskirts of the village through some roundabout way that Zrakkon led us on. I was quite relieved when we got there.

He stopped me on the edge of what seemed to me to be a rock wall that outlined the village. It could not do much else, since it was about a foot tall, but something struck me. I had seen this wall before.

We huddled behind a few trees which, if we were seen, would have probably been comical. "There are only two places, I think, that everyone would be kept," he said. "The stables and the jail."

"Makes sense," I said, although I really had no idea at this point.

He looked up at me with a doubtful look in his eye. I shrugged. He sighed. "I will go to the stables. That is where they might keep the soldiers. You go to the jail and see who is there."

"Okay," I said, thought for a second and then asked, "Where's the jail?"

He made out a crude map in the sand after a bit of huffing and puffing, and showed me. "I'll take Grimmaw with me. I might need the muscle." He added. Grimmaw sighed at that. That made me a little happy.

We parted ways, and I headed into the village. "Try to fit in," he said as I walked away. I was not sure how that would work out, but it was late and most everyone was probably asleep by now, anyway.

Chapter 14

Where's Gerald

I remember that I instantly forgot the directions that Zrakkon had given me. Like they just rattled around my empty skull for a while, making some sort of whooshing noise and then leaving. Though, for some reason, my legs knew the way. I looked at the buildings and they were familiar to me. Not in an 'I know that so-and-so lives here and so-and-so lives there' kind of way, but more of a 'I've been here before, but things are a bit different' sort of way.

No matter the reason how they knew, my legs pulled me as I looked about at the buildings, kind of, but not exactly, in the way they did when Jeff controlled me. I sort of just knew my way around the village. Until I got to the jail.

I was not very sure how I got there, but I did know when I got there because I heard the grandfather's voice through the tiny window. He seemed to be calming down the others, but I was not sure because it was in his goblin language. I started to think how strange that it was that I could understand the humans, and the goblins when they spoke in the human tongue, but not the goblin language.

I went through a few reasons in my head and settled upon, with the basic facts I knew such as that I was the size of a human, knew the language, and seemed to know at least a bit about the village, that I was probably a human. And probably had been to the village at one point or another.

Hold on a minute, though, it gets better, but we'll get to that soon.

Anyway, I was thinking of all these things when a human snuck up on me. By snuck up, I really mean that I was thinking and that I really should have heard him coming and could have easily hidden from him, but I did not do that.

He turned the corner, stopped, and looked at me, and I waved at him.

I am quite sure this was not what Zrakkon meant when he told me to 'fit in'. My hood was still over my head and my gloves were on, so I thought that I may still have a chance to salvage my rescue mission.

"Um, hi," is what I came up with to say.

"Who are you?" Asked the guard. I figured that he was a guard for a few reasons, including that he had armor and a sword and that he was near the jail.

"Um, no one, really. Just out for a stroll," I said. "Nice night, eh?"

He moved closer; I moved back. "Not really the best place for a stroll tonight. Expecting goblins."

"Goblins? Oh my," I tried to sound convincing. I am pretty sure I was not. "They would not dare."

"They may," he said, trying to come closer again. At that, I just pulled my sword and slapped him over the head. It must have been a good hit because he crumpled pretty quick and did not get up.

I backed away from him and hoped he was not dead, but it seemed no one heard me. Well, except the goblins.

They quieted down after the thrump sound of my sword on said guard's head, then I heard a whisper. "Bonesy?" the whisper said.

"Yes," I said.

"Great! How many guards are out there?" the grandfather said, slightly louder so I could tell it was him.

"At least one, but I don't think that he will be bothering us for a while." I kicked at him. There was no reaction. "He might be dead."

"Are there any living ones?" he asked.

"Not sure, but this one has keys." I reached down and pulled the keys off his belt. When I pulled, I saw that his chest was moving. "There's one."

"One what?"

"Living guard, he's still breathing," I replied.

"Great." I heard from someone, but it was muffled.

"You should whisper," he said.

"I don't think that I can," I said, maybe a little quieter, but it definitely was not a whisper.

"Do you think you can get us out?" he asked.

"That depends on if there are more guards."

"Can you check?"

"Sure."

So I did.

I did not have to do much to check as right about then I heard another guard asking 'Gerald' if everything was okay.

He said, "Gerald, what the hells man. You all right back there."

I panicked, "Yup, yup. All good." I assumed the man I bashed in the head must have been Gerald. I kicked him lightly, just to make sure he was still alive. Or maybe just to make sure he would not say anything that would give away that I was not Gerald.

"How long's it take to piss?" The voice asked.

"Just, um, my buckle is stuck. Be there in a minute," I replied.

I went to the tiny window. "I think there's one more."

"We got that," the grandfather said. "Do you think that you can take him out?"

"Not sure, haven't seen him yet. I'll sneak around." I said.

So I did. I moved around the building and looked around the corner. "Hells, Gerald, you need help there," the other guard said. I could not answer now. He would probably figure out that I was way on the other side of the building and was, indeed, not Gerald. He was a pretty big guy, but with some surprise, I thought that I could probably take him out.

We would not find out though, because as chance would have it, Zrakkon took that moment to free the other goblins, creating quite the ruckus. The unnamed guard yelled, "Something's up at the barracks, Gerald! You got this?" but he did not wait for Gerald to answer and he ran off towards the commotion.

I waited a moment to make sure that he was gone and then took that opportunity to look through the keys that I took from Gerald and unlock the door to the jail.

I was hoping that I was wrong and that Grit would be here with the others as the grandfather, some other elderly goblins, and a few younglings exited the door. But no Grit, as I had thought. It seemed as if Jeff had indeed taken her with him.

"Thank you," the grandfather said and took my wrist in greeting.

"But I caused this," I said, my head sinking low.

"Maybe partly," he said, "but not intentionally. Your heart was in the right place. You did not know that this would happen."

"They took Grit," I said.

"Yes, Karrish took her," it was his turn to look down, "I could not stop him."

The name Karrish brought back a memory. I knew that name. It was Jeff. "That name, I knew him once," I said, not really aware of what I was saying.

"Karrish? He is the wizard of the mountain. He's been tormenting us for decades now," the grandfather said.

"I know that name," I said again. The sound of the battle rose. "We have to leave."

A woman's voice came from behind us. "You're not going anywhere," it said.

We turned to see the woman, well-dressed and vaguely familiar. "Mayor, please. We are old or children, we pose you no harm." The grandfather told her, "Let us go."

One guard moved towards him, the other towards me. I raised my sword. "Let them go and I will surrender." I told them.

"Why would we..." the woman began. Another older voice interrupted her.

"Where did you get that sword?" the voice asked me.

"It is mine, or at least I think it is. It was with me when I came back." The owner of the voice came from the shadows and I beheld her. An old woman walking with a cane. Her eyes squinted to see the sword.

"That was my husband's sword," she said.

"Alya?" I asked the woman. She nodded, and then my gaze moved towards the mayor.

My daughter.

Chapter 15

How I Died and Other Revelations

Memories flooded back as I looked from the older woman to the younger. I had never seen my baby; my wife was still pregnant when I went on that 'Easy money' adventure. We had settled down after my adventuring had slowed, and before that, I had retired from the army. We were good. Financially and emotionally. But one more adventure that could maybe put us in a position where we never had to want or need for anything again.

If what my friend had said that my other friend had said was true, the treasure of a dragon would be partially mine.

I am not sure if you know what a dragon has for treasure, but it's a lot. I mean a lot a lot. I mean, more than you truly could imagine. At least, if the legends were true. And maybe they were not totally true, but legends have to come from somewhere, do they not? Someone, somewhere, had to have seen a dragon treasure and told about it.

And if the legends of dragon treasure were even half true, then my portion would be some ridiculous amount of money. Enough, at the very least, to make sure that my child would be set for at the very least, a long, long time.

That, of course, were my thoughts before I got to the dragon's former lair. And after all, I was told that the dragon had left many years ago, and the cave had collapsed. Therefore, fighting a dragon was not on the agenda.

Fighting a dragon would have been at that point in my career, a definite no-no. But, if the dragon was gone...

Those were my thoughts at the time.

My wife's thoughts, as usual when I looked back, were more important. "What if..." she said. And, she said them over and over again.

"What if you are maimed and can't work the farm?" she had asked.

"What if you get trapped?" was another.

"What if you meet someone else?" I had laughed at that one. No one would ever compare to her.

"What if you don't come back?" Which was, of course, followed by:

"What if you die?" That one hit deep. Then? Yes. But especially now, figuring that was exactly what had happened.

Never once did I think that I would find someone else, or willingly not come back. Imprisoned seemed to be a remote possibility. But dying? Adventuring was a dangerous business, even when everything went right.

"It's basically guard duty," I had said. "I'm just watching the door." I touched her belly, where my child and apparently future mayor had been growing.

"Don't go." She said, but she did not actually say the words. It was in her eyes. But, I did not see it then. I do now. And I did as I saw her as a skeleton and her thirty years older. I wish I had seen it then, or that she had said the words. I would not have gone.

But I did not, and neither did she.

And so I kissed her lips for the final time. I think that it is okay to tell you that since you now know that I did indeed die. That suspense is ruined, forgive me. But how I died and how I ended up where I did to be reanimated, you do not know. I wish that it was more exciting, or maybe that I was a better storyteller and could weave a wonderful tale for you, but I must tell it as I remember.

Maybe someday I'll embellish a bit and make me seem a bit less foolish. Maybe a little more heroic. But, for now, I will tell it exactly how I remember it.

So, my friend Bramble came to me one day. I know his name is a bit weird, but he was half human and half elf. And he was not the normal kind of half-elf, or if you will, the accepted kind. Usually if you are half elf, the father is the elf. I'm not entirely sure why that is, but if we thought about it, we probably could figure it out.

Anyway, Bramble had an elven mother and a human father. This was a bit on the weird side among the half elven community and the elven community in general. (Some communities of elves welcomed the human-elf relationship, but not usually in this instance. I don't know, you'd have to ask the elves about it. They are a bit uppity about things being traditional, so you know, that's probably the issue).

Either way, Bramble came to me and told me of this wonderful deal with Karrish. Now Karrish was our cleric. If you are not sure about clerics, we basically keep them around to call on their god to heal us if and usually when we get hurt.

They most likely can get us through an adventure and on to the next town, where we can get some real healing.

We make fun of clerics a lot. And I mean a lot. They sit around and pretend to be useful until someone gets hurt, then they do some sort of mumbo-jumbo and we're ready to fight a bit, get some treasure, and share it with them for helping us keep fighting.

They are, in the adventuring community, the most sought after and also the most ridiculed of everyone. We need them there, but most of the time, they are useless. Depending on the cleric's personality, they also can get pretty preachy about everything. Hells, even when we are in a town just seeing what is going on, they are a burden. Usually finding somewhere to pray or what not and yelling at you about all the unsavory things you do there.

But again, we need them or we'd either have to keep going back to some town to get bandaged up all the time or get killed easily.

It did not help that Karrish really had no people skills whatsoever.

I personally had to bail him out of at least fifteen jams that he had got himself in just by talking. Truthfully, he was lucky that I was married and faithful. Most of our party was just, well, partying, and he probably would have been killed. But I was there.

Turns out I should have let him fend for himself.

So, to get back to the story, Bramble came to me and said that Karrish had found some sort of map of an ancient dragon treasure that had been abandoned.

I said, of course, "What if the dragon comes back?" because if they did, well, that would not be good.

"Can't," Bramble had told me. "The cave collapsed. The dragon can't fit."

I thought about this a bit, as it did make sense. If the dragon can't fit into the cavern, then the dragon probably would move on. 'Sucks to be him,' we might say, and take his treasure.

"Really, Karrish?" I said. Now this should have been the red flag of all red flags. Karrish never, ever had a plan. Wonderful healer, did the job, the personality of a bug, but, well, did a great job. Seemed happy when we paid him. But to come up with the plan? That was weird.

"I'll have to ask the wife," I said. At that point, I was hoping she would just say a quick no and be done with it. But she did the whole look instead of saying no, and I totally misread that. My bad.

I was in.

I'm going to say, that if you have a wife, or husband, or even just a significant other of any sort, when they speak, (or even if they don't and just give you that look that says don't do that, that sounds like a bad idea (you know the look if you've been in any relationship of substance)) you should heed that warning. That information is more valuable than gold.

I did not. I kissed my wife for the last time and threw my pack on, sheathed my sword, and walked out with the stupidest smile I could ever have. I was marching into death and thought I was making the best decision of my life.

To my credit, I did not know that I was going to be betrayed.

So we went, Bramble the elf/ranger, Karrish, our cleric, Me, the fighter, Alleron, our mage, and Riley, the rogue.

Now that I think of it, I am quite sure that Riley was the skel whose foot I knocked off. Now that is a bit of a kick in the ass. I really thought that if any of our normal party would betray us, it would be her. Now I just felt bad for knocking off her foot and hiding her head in the woods.

Either way, we made our way through the woods and to the mountain. As far as we knew (or were told) the mountain was occupied by cobolds. Now cobolds were not much of a threat. They came in large numbers, but as long as you keep your calm, they were easy to scare off. And I mean scare off by killing a bunch of them. They were, however, very smelly.

And if you thought that they were smelly on the outside (believe me, they were) they smelled much worse on the inside. The thing that should have given it away, though, was that there were none. No smell that was. Nor cobolds.

There was no resistance whatsoever. We fought a few giant bugs, a spider was probably the hardest of them, and even that was a joke. I asked Alleron at one point, 'Why are we here?'

He just shrugged.

We entered through a giant door and my reflexes should have told me that something was wrong as soon as the door began to close. I should have yelled for my people to run and run myself, at that point. But...

It was beautiful. I am not sure if you have ever heard of what a dragon's treasure trove would look like, but if you have read about it in various books, it does not do it justice. It may be accurate, but to see it. It's blinding to the mind.

I, for one, was in awe. I can not even imagine what Riley was thinking. Alleron lit up the room with a spell and we had to shield our eyes. The gold, electrum, the diamonds, the swords, and everything else. It was too much for our minds to understand.

The door closed behind us before we even knew what was happening.

That had been my job. To watch the door. My only job. I failed.

The door closed with a bang and another, across the chamber, began to open. I saw Karrish smile from the corner of my eye as he picked up a gem, a large, ruby-colored rock. The look on his face made me shiver. There was a sort of craze in his eyes.

I saw the door open and the goblins rush in.

"Hold the door!" I yelled.

He laughed. He left.

"I remember. I was there," the grandfather said.

Everyone turned to him. "Karrish, or Kallier as he called himself to us, told us that if we helped him dispose of the trespassers," the grandfather pointed at me. "He said that we could have the bounty of the treasure. So we came, and we fought for him."

"They came in and we tried to fend them off, but there were too many." I said, "I tried to organize my group, but Riley went down quick, followed by Alleron."

"He had told us to take out the wizard, described him, even." The grandfather said, "The rest, he told us, would fall with time if the wizard fell."

I remembered watching as Alleron, my friend, was struck down. He took many goblins with him, but there were too many. As I watched him and Riley fall, I looked at Karrish. He held the ruby stone in his hand, his face contorted, his eyes wide. He walked to the door that the goblins had come from. He began to close it.

There was one goblin who saw this happening as we fought the others. He tried to hold the door. At the last moment, he slipped under before it closed on him.

"Yes," the grandfather said as I looked at him. "That was me. I escaped with the wizard, or as you say, cleric."

Everything went dark after that. With Alleron down, the light enchantments were dispelled. As soon as Bramble fell, I heard him scream. I knew that we were done for. He was the only one who could see at all in no light. The only one who could still cast a spell to shine any light.

I remember getting stabbed the first time. I told them of the pain as it sank into my stomach and I felt the blood spill. The second came soon after. I fought on, stupidly or heroically, depending on how you felt about it. I felt five more swords pierce my skin before I fell. The last of the party who had stayed.

The grandfather filled us in on what had happened outside the door. "I followed the cleric to an opening. He held the ruby-colored rock like it was the most precious stone in the world. I felt if I took it from him, I could save my people. He bashed me away without much trouble and left me for dead."

The others must have just died there over time, unable to escape. That is who was reanimated with me.

"They're coming!" yelled the boy with the broken leg. It broke me from my stupor of reminiscing and staring at my wife. She was more beautiful than I had ever remembered. Older, yes, worn with age, but it mattered not. She was the most beautiful thing I had ever seen, now or then.

"Josiah!" I said, actually surprising myself that I now remembered his name. The blonde and brunette were helping him. I wondered when it would be that they would understand that they did not need him at all, but that thought left me quickly.

"Who?" my daughter said. I was quite proud of her demeanor in such a situation.

"Skeletons," the boy managed after catching his breath. "An army of them. Coming straight here."

The blonde butted in. I liked her, and probably should ask her name if the chance ever came about. So far, that chance really had not. "Not just skeletons," she said. Now obviously did not seem like the time.

"I figured as much," my daughter said. "I told the men not to trust them. Tell the army to let the goblins go. We need them for defense."

"Maybe we can help." The grandfather said in the chaos.

"Why would you?" I asked, most likely echoing what others were thinking.

"We may never be friends," the grandfather said to my daughter and took her hand, "But we need not be enemies."

Chapter 16

Off to Find Grit

The grandfather and the mayor (my daughter! I was still a bit star-struck that she was thirty now and in charge of the town, even if it was a small village and she just sent her 'army' per se, to attack my friends. I was still proud, and she did not know they were my friends at the time, or even that I was not so dead, so I gave her a pass) got everyone to stop fighting and get together. It took a while, but eventually, everyone stopped trying to kill each other long enough to listen, even if it was just for a moment or two.

"We need to work together," my daughter said, which was met with a chorus of boos from both sides. "The skeletons..."

The blonde interrupted, "and zombies."

The mayor (my daughter, yes I have to put that in) gave her a look, "and zombies..."

"I just really, really think people need to know about the zombies. They are freaky." She continued.

"And the freaky zombies." She looked at the girl, seeing if that was sufficient. It was not.

"You'll, um..., recognize them," she said with a certain twang to emphasize the word recognize.

"Really?" my daughter (the mayor) asked.

The woman just nodded with a squished-up, almost duck-like expression on her lips.

"Really freaky zombies," the mayor (my daughter) told everyone, "You probably should find a way to prepare yourselves for that," she added.

"And I know that these are indeed the same humans who we just fought, who burned down our village, and who imprisoned us to await some unknown fate." he looked to the mayor who mainly just mouthed another 'really?' at him. He shrugged at her with an 'I have to tell the truth.' type expression. "But if we do not stop this menace now, and maybe find a way to coexist with these humans, then we will either be scattered or destroyed."

I liked that he seemed to take a page out of my book, using the word destroyed.

"We will fight together today, and then go our separate ways." the mayor (again, my daughter, who I may say was very commanding in her speech) said. "Hopefully with better relations and understanding, at the very least."

Zrakkon got to me while I was admiring my daughter, telling all these soldiers what to do and spoiled my 'proud dad' moment. I did find that you could still be proud of your daughter even if you missed the first thirty years of her life and just met her a few minutes ago because you had been dead all that time. It was a dad thing, I guess. "We have to get Grit."

Although I really wanted to keep on seeing this back and forth and see what would come of it, I begrudgingly agreed with him. Except for the 'we' part. He needed to stay here and fight. So I told him, "You need to stay here and fight."

"I am going for my cousin," he said.

"I will take Grimmaw with me and trade myself for her if need be. Jeff, I mean Karrish, wants me for some reason." I told him. "They," I nodded toward the goblins that remained, "need a leader in battle."

He looked at them, to me, and back at them. "Aye," he said. Then he did something I never thought he would. He offered me his hand.

At first I thought that he was going to punch me and I reacted as if he would. Then I realized what he was doing.

"Save Grit." He said.

And so my reunion with my wife, my daughter I had never met, and some strange guy who was overly hugging my wife, whose name or relationship I was yet to discover, was cut short. I was pretty sure that he was my wife's new husband, which, to be honest, really ground my millstones a bit. Couldn't he have waited a day to show up? I get it; I was dead for thirty years. I would have hoped that she would have moved on, but give me a minute, man.

I wanted to narrow my eyes at him, but it loses its effect when you have no face, so I made my goodbyes and went off with a small group of goblins, including Zrakkon.

They were to get me to the other side of the skeleton invaders, where I would then make my way back to the mountain where I was reborn. I was hoping at that point I could detect where Karrish would be.

It was not the greatest plan, but we all figured that the most likely place Karrish's hide-out would be was in the mountains. Without any further information, I'd have to rely on our connection.

I called Grimmaw and went to be on my way when Zrakkon ran over to me. "Find my cousin," was all he said, but the look in his eyes showed true fear. He reached for my wrist and I grabbed his.

"I will do my best. Take care of yourself," I said. The wolf and I made our way through the trees and towards the mountain where I died and was reanimated to save the goblin girl who once spared me, while Zrakkon and his men moved to flank the skeleton army. I saw little hope in either of our paths.

Grimmaw and I made our way through the woods. I figured going back to the skel camp where I had trained what felt like forever ago would be a good place to start. I could retrace my steps back to the cavern, at the very least, and figure it out from there. As we walked, Grimmaw whined towards me. I patted his muzzle. "I know, I feel it too."

Something was following us. In fact, it felt as if two separate parties were following us. At first I thought it was just Jeff/Karrish in my head again. But when Grimmaw made mention of it (well, in his own way) I knew that it was something else.

One I felt was solitary and was tracking behind us. I say 'tracking,' but we were just walking out in the open on a path. I actually thought that if someone caught us, we might get there faster. I would not want to put the wolf in any undue danger, though. Although if I was to be honest, he would probably be fine. I was not all that concerned with the follower.

It was the others that gave me concern.

For one, there were more of them, maybe a half dozen, which told me that they were probably our personal escort from Karrish, the cleric himself.

"Let's stop here a moment and check your leg," I told the wolf, and he flopped himself down. He whined a little as I touched the bandage that was there. "I should not have brought you."

Grimmaw pounced up as if to say, "Screw that, I'm fine."

"Relax," I said and re-bandaged him. "I'm not sending you back. Plus, we need to see if our entourage is truly escorting us."

I sat with the wolf and pretended to continue working on the bandage.

Chapter 17

Brigid

The six walking with us were definitely skels, faithful to their orders to the letter, but as tactful as a snail. They stopped as soon as we stopped and made no attempt at trying to hide it.

The one behind was a bit better, but not trained. They gave up more of their location by continuing when we stopped, actually heading towards the skels. I thought at first it may be Zrakkon, but this being seemed light, and although the goblin was short, he was stocky and armored. The follower had to be small-ish, wearing little to no armor, and barely trained for stealth, if at all.

My mind immediately went to my daughter, but why would she follow me?

I had to be sure, and I had to cut off whoever that was before they ran into the skels. If they weren't very stealthy, they also may not be a trained fighter. I also did not want to alert the skels to their location. If I moved, they would. Our only real choices were to either keep going to the skel camp and see what happened, or go and attack the skels, eliminating the threat.

I looked at Grimmaw's leg and his face. He was not ready for a fight. We needed somewhere for him to rest, but we would be attacked to prevent that? Even if we won, Karrish would undoubtedly just send more.

I did not plan this out well. But, then again, there had not been any time.

Either way, we had to move. And hopefully, the follower would reveal themself at some point before they got themself killed. If, of course, they were friendly. If not, maybe they could take a few skels out for us.

I was pretty sure that they were friendly, though. But I had no idea why.

The wolf rested a few more minutes until I felt that the follower was getting too close to the skels. I was pretty sure that the follower would not be attacked unless they became a threat to the skels, but I could not be sure. Karrish could have also been in my head, so we carried on.

I patted Grimmaw's head and gave him an 'I know, hopefully it won't be much longer look'. It seemed to get through to him and he came along.

Poor guy had been through it. Watched his home burn, got injured, saw his best friend kidnapped (this one I'm guessing. He may not have seen it happen, but he still knew that she was gone) had not slept in at least a day, was probably very hungry, being followed by enemies, and then was accompanying me, someone who had no idea where he was going or how to get there (which seems kind of redundant, how could I have known how to get somewhere if I did not know what there was. Maybe how to find out would had been a better term.)

I felt for him, so I gave him another pat.

We moved on, and the skels and whoever else was there followed. I did not have to worry about where to go; it turned out. At one point, we took a turn to the left, but apparently, the skels did not want us to do that. They moved to that side and slowly got closer until we were on the correct path again.

Whoever had ordered them did a good job. They did not get close enough to engage, just close enough to let us know 'Hey, this is the wrong way, go that way' in not so many, or any, words.

They no longer hid themselves after that, though. Now and then they came into sight and Grimmaw would give them a good talking to. But they did not engage us.

They were, however, now on both sides of us and getting closer and closer. They were funneling us to where they wanted us to go.

We reached the cave more or less by accident. I had seen its opening a bit down the way. It looked to have potential, a smallish entrance, maybe wide enough for two, maybe three skels to get through at a time. Not to fight, mind you, but to get through. I could easily defend it from the skels. I (and them I should add) did not tire. I could keep on fighting, it seemed, at least, for-ever, as long as they did not take me down.

Grimmaw could not. The wolf needed his rest.

If the skels did strike me down, he would have to fend for himself. I did not know the orders that they had for the wolf. Was it 'kill all companions', or just 'kill the skeleton'? If I knew the orders, I could have made a more informed decision.

But they had not attacked the wolf yet. And they had not attacked the follower either. I felt that I was the only target. And the orders to them for me were to get me to whatever place they were trying to funnel us to. If I had a rested wolf, I had a better chance of saving Grit.

I felt that I had to take that chance.

"We get close to that cave, we run," I whispered to the wolf, immediately regretting saying it. For one, the wolf did not understand my language. He did seem to understand the sentiment, but that was different than telling him exactly what to do. Trying to tell him that an enemy was an enemy or to keep still was all well and good. But to actually tell him what to do in the fu-ture seemed like a step above skeleton/wolf communi-cation.

I trusted that he would follow my lead. As I have said before, he was a good wolf.

Leading Grimmaw slightly to the left and closer to the cliff face, the skels on my left backed up a little, giving us what I hoped would be enough room. I patted his mane. "Almost, my friend. Almost."

The right flank came a tad bit closer. I saw the archer remove an arrow from his quiver. I was not very worried about him. As long as he did not hit Grimmaw in a soft spot, then his thick hide and fur would hold up. I looked at the wolf and second-guessed myself. I was not sure if he could run at the moment.

Doubt set in and I almost blew our opportunity.

Then instinct kicked in. I pulled the wolf to the left. "Run!" I yelled.

Any doubt of the wolf's ability to understand quickly melted away. Grimmaw ran straight towards the cave.

An arrow was launched.

It struck him in the backside.

I grimaced a little, but he did not waver. I pulled my sword as the skels began to close around us.

Another arrow swished by me. Or was it?

It was smaller, a bolt from a crossbow. But smaller. Larger than a dart.

It struck the skel nearest me. It did not destroy the creature, but it staggered it.

Another bolt flew by. And another. And another. I had thought that there was only one follower, but the rate of the bolts could not be coming from a single person.

The shots were ineffective in destroying the skels. They were incredibly well-placed shots, however, hitting their skulls and shoulders, distracting them.

I reached the mouth of the cave a few moments after the wolf. Even in his desperate state, he was faster than me. I turned to fend off the assault of the skels, and hope that the follower was safe.

I raised my sword to strike the first thing I saw. I swung. I held up just in time.

The follower was the blonde.

If not for the fact that we were being confronted by mindless skels, I would say that in that cave, we were a fearsome threesome. I had pulled my sword, and the brunette had dropped her seemingly endless ammo crossbow and pulled a weapon more suited to attack skels, a club with a large spiked head on it, from her belt. Behind us, Grimmaw, a large dire wolf just waiting to rip something apart. Drool dripping from his maw. He either wanted to kill something, or more likely, take a nap.

To our surprise, the skels did not attack us. They stood outside, as if on guard, but they did not try to enter. It took us a while, but eventually, we relaxed and Grimmaw took a much-needed nap.

"Why did you follow us?" I finally asked the brunette.

"No, 'thank you'?" she said.

I thought for a moment and then decided to give in. "Thank you. Now why were you following us?"

She sat and removed her cloak, beginning to, what appeared to me, reload her crossbow. I did want to know more about that contraption, but now was not the time. "They wouldn't let me fight the skeletons coming to the town, so I thought that I may of be some use here."

"I thought that you were going to get yourself, and him," I motioned towards the wolf, "killed."

She looked down, took a breath, and closed her eyes.

"But, thank you. You really saved us out there." I felt that since she was here, putting her down was not going to help anyone. Besides, she did help out. "What's your name? I never got it before."

Her demeanor changed almost instantly with my compliment. Nothing like a teenager to change emotion on demand. "You're welcome. My name is Brigid."

"Well, welcome. I'm Bonesy," she looked at me with a sarcastic smile. I raised my hand, "This is Grimmaw."

"Bonesy it is then," she smiled at me. This was quite a different encounter than our first. I mentioned this to her.

"Not really," she said and looked at Grimmaw's leg, "I'm still fighting skeletons."

I looked out to where the skels were. They had formed a semi-circle around the cave entrance and were just standing there. "Last time was not really 'fighting'," I said, looking for a way to close up the entrance a little. "I don't know what they are doing."

"Well, last time was a bit of a surprise." She joined me by the entrance. "I was expecting to go swimming and have a little fun, not be attacked by a skeleton and giant wolf."

"I didn't attack. I was just minding my own business." I gave up on fortifying the entrance and fashioned a seat where I could watch the skels.

"That's not how Josiah told it when we got him back to town," she laughed.

I had to laugh a bit too. "I'm sure. Is he your..." I started to ask.

"Oh no, no," she laughed more. "No, he's more Grace's boyfriend. But, he's fun. Or was. Now he's all whiny and needy with his leg, and all."

I mentioned that I was sorry about that as she sat down next to me. "No worries. He did attack you first. I had told him about the sword thing, but he didn't listen to me. Apparently, it took a skeleton that he never met before to convince him."

We sat in silence for a few minutes and stared out towards the skels. It had started to rain, but it did not faze them. They stood still, water dripping off of them, staring back at us. They were either waiting for us (well, Brigid and Grimmaw) to fall asleep, or waiting for us to make the first move.

Chapter 18

The Tower

For someone for whom time really doesn't matter, I could have sat there forever. One second or one minute or one hour or one day were basically irrelevant to the skels, and mostly to me. They were the same. But, to the living, well, they seemed to try to fill in time, mostly, from what I have seen, by working or talking about the weather.

Brigid kept starting to say something and then stopping. She wanted to fill in the time, but did not know how. She had a persistent tear that she kept wiping away from time to time.

"Why are you really here?" I asked finally. I figured that may be what she needed to talk about, and the skels still weren't doing anything exciting, even with the wolf snoring at a high pitch. Waiting, no matter how much I just wanted to go get Grit, was probably the wisest idea.

I figured that whatever it was, I would get some reaction. I could sense something weighed heavy on Brigid, but could not place it. Her demeanor did not change, however.

She did not say anything at first. I waited her out, although at one point I wondered if she did not hear my question. Then I began to doubt if I had actually asked the question or just meant to. I thought to ask again, or for the first time, if I had only thought that I had asked the first. Then she looked down and sighed.

"My brother was with the attack force against the goblins," she said.

I was unsure why she was telling me this at first, and I began an "Oh, that's interesting," sentence but stopped somewhere between in and esting.

"He did not come back," Brigid said. She did not have to. I had, by that time, figured it out. "I could not stay there and see if he did now."

I did not know what to say. First off, I was not accustomed to helping people deal with grief, because, well, not many people talked to me if they could avoid it. Second, I'd only been not-so-dead for a short time. I had no idea what to do in this situation. So, I did nothing. I just sat with her and waited to see if she would say anything else. After a while, she did.

"I thought that if I could help you, even a little, take down whoever is creating these abominations." She stopped there, looked at me, and said, "Sorry."

"No worries, I get it," I said. I was not lying either. I did understand. Had I been human, or goblin, or anything with skin, to be honest, I would have thought the same. I probably thought that way when I was human. Sometimes, I still did think that way.

"I thought, maybe if I could at least help bring a stop to this madman, this so-called cleric, maybe it could give my brother rest. If he had been..." she tailed off. I did not blame her. "I wouldn't mind getting back at the goblins, either. Or the humans, but..." she tailed off again.

"Why are the humans and goblins fighting each other?" I asked her, "I mean they barely interact, from what I've seen."

"You'd have to ask the elders, those in power, on that one," she told me. "The young people know to hate them, but they don't know why."

"The mayor?" I asked her.

"And others, but yes."

We ended there, oh there was more conversation before we decided that the skels were not going to attack, but it was all just regular human fluff. 'What do you like to do?' and 'What's your favorite animal?' silly things like that.

It was too much for a human for one day and she needed sleep. I, however, stood vigil over the wolf and my new friend, wary of an attack that did not come.

They did not even move. At all.

It was creepy. For a little while, I thought that maybe they had somehow switched off and would not even notice if we walked out of the cave at that moment.

Then I realized that I had not moved at all, in the same amount of time.

I wondered if they had thought the same as me, that I was 'deactivated' or something like that.

Truth was, if they weren't attacking, there was nothing for either of us to do. So we just stared at each other for a few hours or so, which really meant nothing to us, and waited for the living things to wake up. I briefly wondered how the humans and goblins were faring against the attack. It would be nice to get back and talk to my former wife and daughter, which would be tough if they were dead.

It would be a downer if I saved Grit only for her to have nothing to return to.

I spiraled a bit, thinking about these things, but pulled myself out before sinking too deep. There was nothing that I could do about that right now. Wallowing in it would help no one. I wondered if the other skels had the same problem, overthinking.

I guessed not, but I did not really know. Were they stuck in their own heads thinking, but unable to move freely? Where I have that freedom now, were they always tortured as I was in the beginning? Were their thoughts always spiraling? I realized at that moment that I was looking at one of their faces in particular. It looked sad. I touched my own and felt the contours to see if mine were the same. Did others look at me as I did him?

"What's going on?" I heard behind me. Some guard I was.

"Awake already?" I asked her. Still sliding my hand down my face. I could not feel it, really. A bit of pressure, but nothing else. Something was missing.

I did not stop my stare at the skels face. She sat next to me and looked from me to my target, "It's been hours."

"He seems so sad," I replied to her.

She stared at the skel I was looking at for a moment. "You all seemed to look the same to me."

I rubbed my chin, oblivious to her words, and realized that I probably had grown a long beard there at one time. I was not sure why I thought that or how, looking back, I knew that. But now I did. And that intensified my own sadness.

"I think he's waking." I heard her say. I looked back to see Grimmaw, initially just blinking his eyes and wearily looking around. His eyes closed for a second and then he jumped up, growling and running back and forth. I went to him and patted his muzzle.

I felt his muscles calm under my hand.

I patted his head. "Better, my friend?"

The wolf licked my face, which I decided to take for an affirmative, although the thought of him just seeing if I tasted good enough to chew on me did cross my mind.

I could think of a worse fate than being Grimmaw's chew toy.

"Ready to go save our friend?" I said to him. Along came another lick and a bit of a growl. That did not belay my fears of him wanting to bury me for fun.

"You think that they will just let us out of here?" Brigid asked.

"Only one way to find out."

There we were, ready to make our final stand against what I counted to be thirty skels. I can't tell you if it was thirty because I counted a few times and got a different number each time I did.

I think I got twenty-seven once, thirty-two twice, and twenty-nine another. I figured I would split the difference and call it thirty.

It did not really matter at that moment though, there could have been more in the woods waiting, anyway. If the wolf were healthy and Brigid was a halfway decent fighter, I felt we had a shot at taking them. But Grimmaw was not healthy and although the woman may be a great fighter, I had only seen her run from a wolf and shoot bolts from her hand crossbow thing.

I had meant to ask her about that in the cave; it seemed neat. It would have to wait.

So we came out ready. Grimmaw drooling at a chance to pounce. Brigid with her crossbow thing in one hand, her club, spiked-star thing in the other. And me, two hands on my sword and ready to take some skel heads.

To my surprise, relief, and disappointment, the sad skel walked forward, sword sheathed, as the other skels remained motionless. He pointed, quite ominously I'd say, and said in his best Jeff/Karrish voice, "Go." I looked at my companions. Grimmaw was ready, but he had already bled through his bandaged leg.

Brigid was ready too, but something in her eyes told me not to push her, at least not yet.

I nodded and sheathed my sword. Brigid hesitated and looked at me. I put my hand on her shoulder. "Now is not the time." I told her.

She paused. I feared that she would strike for a moment, as the hatred for the skels burned in her eyes. She had turned that gaze on me as well, if only briefly. I tried to give her a reassuring, 'we'll destroy them all later' kind of smile, but with no face, I'm sure something got lost in the translation.

Regardless, she hooked her crossbow and club thing onto her belt. The skels led us silently through the woods. It seemed not to be far from where I originally met up with Grit and Grimmaw. The terrain began to become hilly, and the trees started to thin out. We were close to the small village area where I received my initial training.

"What is that?" Brigid asked me and pointed. I looked through the trees, at first not picking it up. Squinting would have come in very handy at that point, and I did try to, embarrassingly, a couple of times.

"A tower?" I answered with my own question.

Her eyes were wide. "I don't remember anyone ever mentioning a tower out this way. Do you?"

I thought for a moment. I remembered my time there, not long, but I had nothing to do except look around at everything. "There wasn't one." That was all I could say.

We looked ahead and saw where the training village had been. What once was a thickly wooded area was now where the tree line ended abruptly. The land was scorched. What we had seen as a tower through the trees was more than that.

Much more.

A stone wall had been erected where my training ground had once been. Thirty feet tall at its shortest. It stretched as far as I could see to the north. To the south, it rose into the hills towards the mountain. The tower, well towered over it, with hints of a castle being built inside.

Brigid just looked at me, wide-eyed, mouth agape.

Chapter 19

City of the Dead

The size of the wall and tower was stunning. We were led by the skels through the massive gates and a double wall, with a ten-foot pass way in between. The pure scale of this fortress was astonishing. To be created in such a small amount of time seemed impossible, at least until we got through the second gate.

There were thousands of skels working on the construction. Now I had a bit of trouble with the thirty, mainly just because I was counting all willy-nilly, but I was not even going to try and count these, but everywhere you looked there were skels.

Stones were being brought from the mountain, shaped, and then installed. Skel horses, wolves, and oxen maybe, carrying load after load.

So many were newly dead. Like zombies that rose from their fresh graves.

I even shuddered at the sight. Brigid threw up. She said the stench, which was probably part of the truth. The sight alone made me wish I had had a stomach to purge. She was looking for a way to bolt from the 'City of the Dead' but the gate had closed.

Grimmaw even seemed to be sickened by all of it.

The sad skel led us to the castle, which itself was massive, sporting the giant tower in its center. A moat, which I think I remembered seeing as a pond that was fed from the mountains, surrounded it. A drawbridge lowered for us, adorned with skulls on the top.

"Enter," he said and stood to the side.

"Where are we going?" Brigid asked, but the sad skel was finished. He just stood there unmoving, untalking. His job was done. She waved her hand in front of him, but he did not waver. She feigned a punch, but he did not flinch. "What the Hells is going on?" she asked me.

I shrugged. I had no idea. My only hope was that Grit was in these walls and that we could somehow survive this.

It was, you can probably imagine, a fleeting hope. There were too many. If they all attacked at once, we'd be destroyed in seconds. I regretted at this point not trying to fight our way through when we exited the cave. But looking back now, I can not really see how it would have helped even if we had won.

The entrance led to a grand hall with tables that could seat hundreds. There were indeed hundreds of skels propped up in seats and posed in ways to show a grand feast. These, at least for now, were stationary. Some held turkey legs, though either rotted or bone.

All had goblets of wine or mead, spoilt, but still smelling of their former selves.

Some were posed on the dance floor, in a macabre waltz, frozen forever. Or not. As we walked by, I felt them looking at me. I felt their desire to either attack or be free from their prison of undeath.

It was then that I felt that they all, or at the very least, some, knew their fate. Like, when Jeff/Karrish had taken control of me and I struck that skel or almost destroyed Grit upon our first meeting. I knew what I was doing, but could not stop myself. These skels were watching us, wondering why I, alone, could walk freely.

That was the moment it became more than just saving Grit; although that was still the main goal. These poor souls needed to be saved as well. And those outside. And those who may be fighting the goblins and humans at that moment.

"Bakor," I heard a familiar voice, although I could not place it. "It has been far too long."

"He had told me that it was you," the owner of the voice said. "I could not believe him."

I had nothing at that point. The name struck me as familiar, but not my own. "It's been, what? Like thirty years?" I replied. I figured since I had been dead at least that long, I was good with the thirty years guess.

"Must be," he said, then repeated, "must be. Time sure flies when you're dead, though, I bet."

"Like it never happened." I said. Brigid looked at me. I shrugged at her. I had no idea what the Hells was going on. "One day I died, next I'm looking like this." I did a horrible twirl.

"My Gods, I can't believe that you're back!" the guy with the voice said. "Where are my manners? Come. You must all be tired."

He turned, paused a bit, then turned back to me. "Except you, huh Bakor? You don't really get too tired these days, huh?" then laughed way too loud.

"Nope, not really," I said, trying to return the laugh. It came out sad though. I needed to work on it.

He turned again as I shrugged at Brigid another time. She had to be confused. I mean, I had no clue what was going on at all, but at least I had gotten used to that. She was new to all this nonsense.

Grimmaw, to his credit, just went with the flow. Although I was pretty sure that he just wanted to destroy something. And this guy was tops on the list.

"So, I can get the livings something to eat if they're hungry." He looked at Brigid. She stared, coldly, back at him. Her look impressed me. I had not known her (or anyone else for that matter) all that long, but most of what I had seen I liked, "or a bed if tired."

He waved toward a couple rooms at the top of the staircase that he had led us up and then continued to what seemed to be a more formal dining room. "Here, my servants can serve you most anything you desire." He clapped and a few of the skels who had, to that point, been motionless, moved to pull out a chair for

Brigid. She looked at me, but did not move. Apparently, through no fault of my own, I had been elected leader.

I looked to Grimmaw, and as if reading my mind, he bowed his head.

"We," the man with the familiar voice said, "Have a wee bit to talk about, don't we?"

I felt that, at this point, shrugging was definitely off the table as a response to the woman and the wolf's looks. Then, of course, I shrugged yet again.

"Is the food, like, you know, edible?" Brigid asked, breaking the quite awkward silence.

"Of course, of course. You didn't think that I, Bakor's old friend, would serve you rot, did you?" He replied.

"Of course not," I fake laughed, trying to make it sound as real as possible. I looked at Brigid and waved my hand a little. I tried to contour my face to display the point that I thought this guy was totally mad. This is difficult without facial features, but she seemed to get it. She laughed too.

"We'll let these two eat and we can go talk in private a bit," he said to me, "as old friends."

"Sure, sure," I said. I waited until Brigid accepted the seat and seemed at the very least slightly okay with it. Grimmaw found a spot in the corner and lay, keeping a watchful eye on everything.

"Just one thing though," I said.

He turned to me, "Yes?"

"Who the Hells are you?"

"Bakor, you must be joking," He laughed and carried on as if I did not just ask the question. He turned back to Brigid. "Eat, eat. I promise the food will be fine. And some of the best you have ever had, if I don't say so myself!"

He laughed a wild laugh and made his way through the door. I looked back at the blond woman sitting there. She gave me a 'you think I should? This is weird' look with her face. I try to give a reassuring look, but I was sure it did not come off very confident. The wolf was resting in the corner, but on alert. I turned and followed the man through the doorway.

"You should not have come here," the man said as soon as the door was closed. "You're all he needs."

"Look man, I don't know who..." I tried to say, he cut me off.

"I don't know how long I have. I shut him out, but he'll figure it out and break through, eventually." The man said, "You need to run. Run far and run fast. Take your friends, or don't, I don't care. You need to get out of here as fast as you can. I think that I can hold—"

"I don't even know who you are," I told him. "I'm here to get Grit, the goblin girl. Then I'll leave."

"You can't," he said, sat himself down, and poured a drink. Out of, I assumed, courtesy, he offered me one. Out of some respect, I just declined and did not point out how I was a skeleton, and drinking was a bit impossible. "I joined him that day because he promised me much. So much." He paused and took a drink.

I looked at him. I still was not sure who he was, but it was starting to sink in.

"It kept becoming more, and more, and more, and more," He slammed the bottle onto the great oaken table. The drink flowed out of the top and spilled across. He took another shot. "It became this," he waved his arms around.

I looked around. I mean, it was a good room, great even. Then I realized that he meant all of it. The castle, the tower, the wall, the thousands of dead. An army of dead. "He wants you," he said.

"Why?" I asked.

"Eternal life," was all he said. He took another shot and laid his head down. "I swear, Bakor, I did not know that he meant to kill you all. I just thought that he wanted the stone. It spiraled from that day."

It came back to me then, more about how I died. "Alleron?" I asked.

He just nodded.

"He needed you to open the cavern. You read the runes," I said.

He nodded again.

"And he needed Bramble to read the map," I continued.

"He was the only one of us who knew the elvish tongue," he said and took another shot.

"And Riley to disarm the traps?" I knew the answer.

Alleron nodded again.

I thought this through. They all made sense, not the betrayal at the end, but the skills needed to get to his treasure. "Why me?" I asked.

"I did not know at first, I swear," Alleron said. He was almost pleading with me to believe him.

"Why me?" I asked again.

"I swear, you must believe me," he said.

"You joined him after. Why me?" I asked one more time and rose from my seat.

"I did not know it would come to this," he said.

"Why Me?" I yelled. He took everything from me, my life, my wife, and my kid. I threw the sham of a goblet across at him, struck him in the head.

Alleron cowered. "You would have tried to stop him," he said, whimpering. "Probably the only one who would."

Chapter 20

Pull Me Back In

"I was out! Retired!" I rose and must have looked ferocious as Alleron, who I now remembered some of, was a formidable mage in my time, shook and cowered at my visage. In the past thirty years, I would assume he must have grown in power, but here he was in tears. "I had a family, a life. You all brought me back in just to... what?"

"To get the ruby." He said. He backed himself into a corner of the room. I could tell he was preparing something, but if he wanted to attack me, he would have already. I could not push him further without a fight. "It was about the ruby in his staff, some sort of..."

"For a rock?" I yelled.

"It's much more than a rock..." he started.

I forced myself to calm down. Even if I could destroy my former friend, and I hated to admit this, I may need his help to get to Grit and save Brigid and the wolf. "What about you? He wanted the rock, but what did you get for betraying your friends? Dominion over this... city of the dead?"

"I never wanted this," he said, rising to his feet. Alleron seemed satisfied that I would not attack him, at least not yet. "This is an abomination. I wake up every day in this nightmare. Hoping somehow it will be gone. But it is always worse. I wanted power, prestige, a legacy. But no, not this. This is Hell."

"A fair trade for betrayal," I said.

He sat back at the table and contemplated this. "You must run now. My spell shutting him out is weakening."

"I can't," I said, sitting back in my seat.

"It's too late," Alleron said. "You are, he said, the secret to eternal life. If you go there, he may be able to achieve his goal."

I remembered. Alleron did not fall, although in my head, originally, it seemed that way. Especially after what Grit's grandfather had said. I looked at the wizard, in the battle. I was struck in the gut with a sword, and attacked by five goblins. One got through. I had looked to my mage for help. He gave none. He extinguished his light, surrounded by goblins, that at first I thought were attacking him. They were, instead, protecting him.

I wanted to draw my sword and kill him right there. He had betrayed us, his friends. And for what? That I did not know yet. "I need to save my friend. She saved mine. Or at least, whatever this is."

Alleron sighed. I could see the defeat on his face. He wanted me to run, but he knew the old me, the living me, the one who would not run when there was a fight for what was right. I did not know this. He actually knew me better than I did then. I would risk everything to save my friend.

"Very well," the wizard said. "He awaits you in the cavern."

"My friends?" I asked.

"I can get them through the walls. From there, they will be on their own," he told me. "I promise nothing, but I owe you my life to try."

I believed him. Maybe I should not have given my new revelations, but it did not matter much. I had no real choice. I had to save Grit, and Grimmaw and Brigid need not die in vain.

"How do I get to him?" I asked him.

His face dropped, "I hope that you reconsider. If he can harness whatever makes you different..."

"How?" I said.

"He said that he wants you to climb," Alleron said. "If you go any other way, he'll kill the goblin."

My first thought was 'Hey, there's a tower. I'm going to have to climb a bunch of stairs to get to Grit and Karrish.' If you were thinking along those same lines, you would also be wrong, just like I was.

I was not going to be climbing the tower; I was climbing the cliff.

"But, why?" I asked Alleron, who seemed to be feeling a bit more comfortable that I was not about to attack him.

"So the wolf won't come with you," he told me. "I'm not sure that he knows about the girl."

That was good. If he did not know about her yet, then she and Grimmaw had a better chance of escape. But if he could see through the skels, why did he not know that she was there? I felt asking this directly would not get me much information. "Can't he just have the skels keep them here?"

"I think," the wizard began, then paused and rubbed his beard, much like I pretended to, seemingly trying to decide if this was something that he should tell me or not. Eventually, he made a 'what the Hells' sort of face and continued. "Giving them simple instructions and letting them continue doing the same thing over and over seems to be simple for him. Even a more advanced command like, say, 'have the bone-man and the wolf come to the Grand Hall,' is not very difficult."

"But to interact directly, order them, or control them even..." I began.

"Is very taxing." Alleron sat back, much more relaxed. "Therefore, I am sure that I can get your friends to safety. Between attacking the humans and dealing with you, if you still choose to go..."

He paused, with his eyes enlarging just a little. "I am," I said, again to his displeasure.

"Unfortunate," he said. "He should be too distracted to truly direct the 'skels,' as you call them. We should have little resistance."

"We?" I said.

"I have long lusted to remove myself from Karrish's service. You may find a way to stop him. I fear, however, that the odds are in favor that he may use you to become immortal." He looked down, fear building in his eyes. "That I can not be here for. That I cannot stand."

I looked at him. He truly was scared of this fate. "Come help me then." I pleaded. "Let us together stop him."

For a moment, just a brief one, I thought I saw a glimmer of hope in those eyes. Then it was extinguished. He was a beaten man. "No, no. I will have the same fate as you. And I do not envy your fate, my friend."

I thought to chastise him for having the moxie to even think of calling me 'friend' after his betrayal so long ago. I rose and looked into those eyes. The hurt, the shame, and the regret burned in them. I, through all that I lost, my family, my life, and the uncertainty of my fate, did not envy him at this point. Even though I had lost, and lost everything, he was a broken man.

"Help my friends, and your debt to me is paid. Run if you must. Hide from Karrish. But if you hear that I am successful, come back to me and help celebrate our victory." I paused and was hesitant to say the last part, but I added, "Friend."

"You can't..." he began, but quickly put a finger to his lips with one hand and one to his ear with the other.

I understood that Karrish was in his head again. "Where must I climb?" I asked him.

Chapter 21

I Hope Odem is not a Skel

We went back to the others, and I asked him to stay behind a second while I talked to Brigid. I told her about getting her and Grimmaw out of there and the whole climbing thing. "That seems a bit strange." She said.

"What part?" I asked her.

"Well, the whole climbing thing, couldn't he just tell you to not bring Grimmaw? He'd, you know, kill Grit if you brought him." She said. "It's not like you're going to get tired or anything. It makes no sense."

I had not thought of that. "Yeah, I don't know. It is a bit weird. Maybe something from my past that I can't remember."

"You really had some messed up friends. I mean a cleric who raises the dead to create, well, whatever the Hells you call this place." She turned to look at Alleron. "And then this guy. I mean, you want me to trust someone who helped have you killed thirty or so years ago? I'm not buying it."

I had to admit that she made some really good points, and if Karrish did not have Grit, I probably would have listened more. "I'm out of ideas. I have to save Grit and I don't want you or Grimmaw to die. Do you have a better idea?"

"So, the best plan so far is that you, a skeleton who seems to have been some sort of adventurer..." Brigid began.

"And I think military person." I interrupted.

"And maybe military person, although we're not sure and definitely not sure how experienced." She looked over to me for confirmation. I nodded, and she continued, "is going to climb a mountain and fight a cleric, who knows this skeleton's skills, I assume."

She looked at me, "Probably, yes," I admitted.

"And has, as far as we know, pledged his soul to Orcus, Lord of the Seven Hells." I was quite impressed with this. I don't remember anyone bringing that up, but with the whole 'army of the dead' thing going on, that is a pretty good assumption. "Who also, as I understand, has some strange magic rock that gives him more power?"

"Seems correct," I told her.

"And he needs you," she pointed at me to emphasize this, I guess, "to become immortal, or something like that."

I nodded.

"Is that all?" Brigid asked.

"Seems about right," I said. Now before she spelled this all out, I figured that I had about a fifty-fifty chance of maybe pulling it off. Then she said all these things. Now I'm not saying that what she said was wrong in any way, but as a pep talk for me, it lacked in, well, everything. "I mean, when you put it like that..."

"Put it like what?" she seemed upset now. "There is literally no other way to put it. You are going to go up there and then he's going to do some magic, or prayer ritual stuff, and then you'll be dead again and he'll be immortal. Grit will die. Grimmaw will die. I will die. Most likely, that traitorous loser will also die. Then everyone. Will. Die!"

"When you put it like that," I said, "It seems like a rather bad plan."

"It is a bad plan," she said.

"I just, really, don't have another one," I told her, looking at my boots, wondering a bit about my lost toe. "I have to try to save her."

"Why?"

I thought about this one. Why did I care so much about this little goblin? "Grit, and the wolf, and maybe her grandfather, and Odem..."

"I don't know Odem," she interrupted.

"Not important now, plus he's already dead," I thought about that for a second and hoped that he was not a skel now, maybe fighting the humans. That would not be good. He'd not be on board with that at all. "Are the only people who saw me as more than just a skel."

Chapter 22

The Climb

"Fine," she said. I could tell that it was definitely not fine, at least that is what I got from her tone. It was more of the type of fine where the person you are talking to just wanted to end the conversation and be done with you. She accepted it though, and went along with the plan.

Or so I thought.

So I left my former (maybe still), new (maybe), and current (well he's a wolf, so it is a bit hard to tell) friends and went to the cliff to climb up to my fate.

I looked up.

I am not exactly sure how far it was from the base of the cliff to where I needed to get to (Alleron tried to point to the spot, but I think I got a little vertigo, or a lot, I really had no idea) and I just said, "Hells."

"Yup," is all he said and patted my back. He then went to try to prepare the girl and the wolf.

Although I dreaded my next journey of the climb, I did not envy the wizards task. I had told Grimmaw to listen to Brigid, and that she would know what to do, but I was quite sure that the wolf would not leave willingly without Grit. I was also quite sure that Brigid would not leave without me.

I was not sure why I felt that way, but I definitely was sure that it had more to do with the mad necromancer creating thousands of skels living forever than it had to do with my safety. And I certainly got that. I did, however, hope that even just a small part had something to do with my safety.

Whichever way she felt, I had to, at some point, climb. And the skels to the left of me, and the skels at the right, seemed to want this to happen sooner rather than later. So I indulged them and tried. And failed. And failed again.

And again.

"I'll get there," I said to the closest skel. I felt that he looked annoyed, but he looked like he always did.

And again.

"I guess I was not a climber in my previous life," I laughed to him. I imagined that inside his head, he was cracking up at my lame joke. Maybe he was a climber and wanted to give me some sort of tip or something. I hoped that I had at least given him the tiniest bit of joy.

Probably not. But it did give me a bit of confidence.

Brigid's rant broke me a bit. Maybe more than a bit. "A bite." I said and laughed again, patting the skel on the shoulder. He obviously did not get this joke, as I did not say half of it out loud, but I did think, for a second, that he could hear me.

I then thought that he thought, 'please get this guy out of here.' Maybe he didn't think this, but my thought was that he *may* have thought it, and that thought made me think that I had to try to save them.

That if these skels were not just horrible monsters and maybe simply tortured souls. I had to. And yes, I know that I kind of sort of said this before, but at that moment, when I had this skel falling down with laughter over my horrible joke, was when I truly made up my mind.

I was going to climb that mountain! I ran up to it, jumped up, and tried to hang on.

And again, I slid right down.

"Hold on, buddy. Don't you give up on me," I said to the skel, as he stared blankly at me, giving me the courage that I needed. "I got you."

Climbing was not all that bad once I got the hang of it. Being just bone, I was pretty light, and as long as I could find some sort of grip, I was alright. I got about twenty feet up and yelled down to the skel, "I got it now. Look at me go."

Then I slipped a bit, not like I was going to fall or anything, but enough to try to forget about the skel and concentrate on climbing.

I don't know about those people who climb for fun, if I were alive and did not have to, I'd skip it, but to someone who is not really into this sort of thing, it becomes both terrifying and boring at about the twenty-five foot mark. All the power to those who like it. I am not trying to put your exercise or hobby down, but man, I just wanted it to be over at that point.

And I had at least eighty more feet to go.

Then I ran into trouble. Not trouble with the climb, that was just a stabilize, find a hold, pull yourself up, stabilize, repeat. For anyone with a body besides just a skeleton, that might be tough. For me, it was rote.

No, the trouble was mental exhaustion. I talked about spirals before and how the mind can go to infinite places when bored. That was what happened then. Here's the basic track that my mind went to:

First, was Alleron going to be able to get Brigid and Grimmaw out of the city of the dead? Which led to Brigid's rant about the hopelessness of my journey. Which then led to the absolute desolate feeling of this being a totally useless journey. To then feeling as if I would get to the top and be instantly killed, or whatever amounted to being killed in this whole not-so-deadness I was in. Which led to a song that was stuck in my head, but I did not quite know the words. I tried to hum it out, but just kept singing 'watermelon' to most of the lyrics. Which led me to try this in many other songs which I did know and found that it fit quite well in all of them. Which then led to the sadness at the thought that I would never taste watermelon (or anything else, for that matter) again. Which led to my anger that this Karrish guy hung my fellow skels out to dry and that they would never again taste anything, or be able to move or anything without some jerk telling them to. Which led to me looking down to the skel to tell him that I would make things right, only to find that I was now about seventy-five feet up and maybe, in my previous life, might have been afraid of heights. To the realization that I was almost finished with my climb and that I was probably about to find out what 'dying' meant when you were already dead.

I stopped myself there and felt the rock under my right hand break from the wall. I caught myself but watched as the rock fell all the way to the ground and struck the skel that I had been talking to in the head.

He did not move. He did not flinch. If I had not seen the rock fall all the way from my hand to his head, I would have thought that I imagined the whole thing. In a way, I still did. Poor guy probably now had a hole in his skull.

I would have, if I could have, taken a deep breath. This was it. No turning back now.

I reach up and over the ledge.

Chapter 23

I Don't Like the Sound of That at All

I took a look down before pulling myself up and wondered that at this height what could be left of me if I fell. Clearly, I would not be reduced to dust, probably shattered pieces.

Could I control those pieces as I did my detached arm? Create different forms of all the pieces of my skeleton?

It was actually fun to think about as I dangled there with one arm looking down. What could I become? Obviously, I was not going to try it, as it seemed like a pretty big gamble. I might just have to lie there forever doing nothing. Maybe a bird would come by and take my finger for his nest.

That train of thought led me to lament the loss of my middle toe.

I had almost forgotten about my toe on many occasions. I mean, a lot of stuff had happened between losing the toe and climbing this cliff. And it was not like I actually needed it, did I?

But it tugged on me somewhat. I could still feel it sitting out there. I had to try to remember to get it if I could after this ordeal.

I looked up to where I was pulling myself, and then I saw it. The stupid, large, ruby-colored stone. It was attached, as I saw pulling myself up a bit more, to a staff that was, of course in the hands of Karrish (formally Jeff, if you haven't been keeping up, or if you skipped ahead or something, or just forgot).

"Bakor! You have finally joined me!" he said with a stupid grin on his stupid face.

"Sorry to keep you," I said and looked up at him, thinking that he might just smack me over the head and make me fall all the way down again. "I would have been here sooner if your skels had not made me climb this cliff."

He did not smack me. He actually just turned and walked away as he said, "Well, I wanted a bit of alone time without your friends here to interrupt us."

"Oh good," I said, standing after pulling myself to the top of the ledge. "We can let her go then."

He looked to Grit, who was at this time in a cage that was dangling over what I supposed was a deep cavern. "Oh no, no, no," he just laughed.

"I'm here. You don't need her," I told him.

"Ironic," he said, finding his way to a stone throne that somehow did not look out of place in the cavern. "Goblins killed you in life and now you have come here, knowing full well what it means for you to save one. Your honor was always so... predictable. The girl stays. She is my insurance that you cooperate."

"What does he mean?" Grit yelled from her cage, "What is he going to do to you?"

I just turned to her and shrugged. I really had no idea. I literally just came to save Grit, and now apparently I have some task to do or torture that he had planned. It was all quite confusing.

"You really don't know?" Karrish asked me.

"I'm not exactly sure how I could," I said.

"I thought you, of all people, would have figured it out. We had talked about this." Karrish stood up from his throne and moved towards me. Not threateningly, but I pulled my sword, just in case.

"I am not exactly a 'people' now, am I? Plus, I just remembered who I was, well, a little of who I was a day or two ago. Before that, I was calling you Jeff." I turned my body and raised my sword.

"Yeah, where did you come up with Jeff, anyway?"

I looked over his shoulder and saw Grit looking towards me. She smiled, which made me want to smile. Luckily, I could not, because that would have definitely given it away. So I looked back at Karrish while Grit attempted to swing her cage. I did not know how that would help anything, but I went with it.

"I don't know, you look like a Jeff," I said.

I totally stopped paying attention to Jeff/Karrish at that point, although I do recall that he seemed mad at my comment. I just concentrated on keeping him talking with a well timed 'oh yeah,' or 'oh right, that makes sense,' every now and again. That, along with a lot of nodding and attempted smiling. I think, for the most part, that my 'I am definitely listening to you while not actually listening to you' skill was pretty good. Maybe I was a politician before. Or a teacher.

As Grit was swinging and Jeff/Karrish was talking (he seemed to love to talk, especially about himself) I kept looking at his staff. Mostly at the ruby on his staff. I couldn't help but be drawn to it. Mostly, I think, because I was killed because of it. But maybe because its power seemed to call to me.

I interrupted him, which I found he did not like. Especially when he was talking about himself. "What's with the ruby?" I asked.

"What?" he said and some sort of lightning thing flew from said ruby into my chest and, for the first time since I became not-so-dead, I felt pain.

"The ruby," I said, wincing from the blow, "Why is it so important that you had to kill three of your friends?"

"Friends?" he said and threw another of those lightning things at me. Think that if you had not felt pain, or really anything for that matter, in the last thirty years and then, bam! The worst pain ever. Well, to be honest, I have no idea about that. I did not remember pain until then. I did kind of remember that there was a feeling that was pain, just not the actual feeling of it. I am sure getting stabbed over and over again by goblins was quite painful, now that I thought about it.

I was in shock. I fell quite close to the edge of the cliff that I had just climbed. Looking over, I saw the skel at the bottom. He was a tiny little skel from this height. I waved, although I am pretty sure that he did not see me.

"How were any of you, *my* friends?" Karrish said. I had forgotten about him in my pain. I mean, I actually really forgot that he was there at all, until he started talking again.

"I tried," I said. Although I was not totally sure if I did or not.

"And I had told you of my plan to find the Staff of Orcus," he said. Anticipating that he was about to send another one of those lightning things at me, I rolled up like an armadillo. I did not really think that it would help any, but did it anyway. "You laughed at me."

"Sorry," I said meekly. Trying to close my eyes, that task, of course, failed.

"It matters not," Karrish said, and he went to his altar. A book (I guess that it is called a grimoire, as I was told later by Alleron) sat at a podium and he turned the pages of the ancient-looking tome. "You seem to hold the secret to ever-lasting life that I have been looking for all these years. I must complete my prayer."

I tried to move towards him, doubly to benefit him not saying this prayer thing and being distracted from the fact that Grit was swinging at a rate that almost had her cage doing a 360 spin, and her laughing almost uncontrollably.

Unfortunately, moving was very, very painful at that moment.

Grit seemed to be having the time of her life, swinging over the crevice that her cage hung until she wasn't. The chain broke as I tried to right myself through the agonizing pain and Karrish tried to find the correct passage in whatever the Hells book he was reading from. She, luckily, came crashing down on my side of the gap, instead of falling into it and probably dying.

The cage was not so lucky and burst into thousands of bits. I did not care much about it, but did say, "oh," and looked in its general direction.

Grit was free! I hoped that she would now run away and then I could find some way to escape as well..

Unfortunately, she did not. Not even close, really. I am pretty well sure that the thought of running did not cross her mind at all.

It was like she just had no intention of saving herself and ran straight at Karrish. I did admire her gumption, and in the wake of my really bad plan, I couldn't really yell at her or anything. But she didn't even have a weapon or anything. We found out just how bad of an idea it was when Karrish said some sort of gibberish again and then she was lying beside me, seemingly in more pain than I was.

That's saying a lot, since I was in quite a lot of pain.

We were, not to be too risque, screwed.

"I think, my friends," that word seemed to flow around here like nobody's business, "that we no longer need the goblin."

I did not like those words one bit, although I held out hope that he meant to let her go. However, I did not think so as it seemed quite ominous, the way he said. Then the pain went away. I was elated for me, but Grit seemed to still be in it. I also was rising to my feet, which I would have said was a good thing, but I was not trying to. Did not think of it at all.

The ruby glowed and called to me. I was up. Believe me, I definitely tried to stop myself, but Karrish was all laughing and saying "destroy" again and I was standing over my friend.

I was also raising my sword.

Karrish stopped saying destroy and laughed some more, then went back to his book. Grit writhed in what I was well aware was horrible, horrible pain, and could not defend herself. Or even move out of the way. A little roll would have helped, but she could not.

The necromancer seemed satisfied that everyone was in place, Grit lying on the ground in front of me, me standing above her with my sword above my head ready to strike her, and him standing in front of his book saying a bunch of things that I could not understand. A strange glow seemed to come from the chasm that Grit almost fell in, a dark green with a tinge of red. It was quite pretty, in a very scary kind of way.

"What ya doing?" I asked. Thankful that I could still talk.

He did some sort of grunt towards me, making me feel as if I may be interrupting him. Naturally, I asked again, "Some sort of spell or something?"

The pretty glow died down a bit, which made me feel a little sad. "I need intense concentration here. You don't want to know what happens if I get this wrong."

"What happens if you get it right?" I asked. I knew that would be bad for me. And probably Grit too.

He looked at me, then shrugged. I guess to him it did not matter if I knew now, "I will devour your soul, which should give me immortality. And your friend there..." He stopped at that.

"And my friend there?"

"She will be sacrificed to Orcus, and I'm assuming, will be tortured for eternity."

"Well, I don't like the sound of that at all," I said as he continued his chanting.

Chapter 24

A Tug of War

I did not see or hear Grimmaw before he struck me, rolling me to my back and then keeping me prone to the floor. That familiar drool dripping onto my face. My sword, the lot good it did me, fell from my hand and teetered over the cliff for a moment, flapping up and down a bit like waving 'goodbye' and then taking a plunge off. Hopefully not destroying any skels that may be loitering away down there.

I heard Brigid's crossbow fire, along with some ping-ping noises, making me aware that Karrish did not get hit by any. I also kept hearing him spouting off some gibberish that I assumed was the prayer he had started.

Then I heard another voice, chanting more gibberish. I assumed that this was Alleron. I was correct in my assumption, but I still was not sure if he was on our side or not.

Then I heard Karrish yell. Not a prayer-like yell, more of an ouch-type yell.

I tried to look over, even with the wolf on me, and saw a bit of the battle. It looked like between Brigid and her spiked mace and Alleron with what seemed to be very pesky spells. We were winning for the moment.

Grimmaw kept looking towards the battle, maybe trying to decide if he should join in, to Grit, who was still in, from her groaning, immense pain, and me. When he looked at me, he growled quite menacingly. "I couldn't help it," I tried to tell him, but he did not seem to believe me. Or at least not enough to get off of me.

I did not blame him at all. He was, as I have said before, a good wolf.

The battle started to become a bit more explosiony, with many more grunts and ahh's! accompanying said explosions. I did feel the explosions, or at least the shock of them, along with some flashing lights. It seemed that the tide was turning, and I heard the footsteps of the skels coming.

I hoped that my recent communing with them may have swayed them to our side, but from the sounds of battle, along with the persistent and all too familiar "Destroy!" command, I was doubtful.

The wolf got a bit more confused as to what to do, which is not surprising. He could get off me, but for all he or I knew, I would just attack Grit.

Speaking of, I looked at my goblin friend again, hoping the pain was gone now. It was not, but it did seem to be less debilitating. She was trying to tell me something. "Gedasti," she managed.

If I could have, I would have given her a very confused and concerned eyebrow motion. Of all the everything that I missed from life, I really never thought missing eyebrows would be one.

"Get, ta, sti," she said again. With a little more pauses. It seemed like words now. I tried to sound it out.

"Getta sti?" I said. She shook her head, "Get tasti?" That wasn't it. I decided to slow it down.

"Get?" the goblin nodded.

"Ta?" her head went side to side. "The?" I corrected. She nodded as furiously as she could.

"Sti?" She looked at me with the eyebrows that I wanted to make earlier. I was jealous.

"Kah?" she said.

"Sti kah?" I said. She nodded.

"Get?" she nodded again. "the?" again, "sti kah?" and again.

"Get the stick!" I said and yelled to Grimmaw, "Get the stick, boy! Go get the stick, bring it back!"

Grimmaw, looked at me, ears up. I motioned a throw, which probably did not help from my position and arm angle. He looked to Grit. "Get it, bring it back."

Grimmaw was off me and running towards Karrish.

I still could not move, even after the wolf got off of me. I looked at Grit and she gave me a 'What are you doing?' kind of look. I tried to shrug, but it didn't work.

Karrish was laughing now, so I was pretty sure that he was winning. The sounds of the skeletons walking and swords swinging only reinforced that idea. Then I heard the wolf's chomp on the staff, Karrish's curse at him (calling him a mutt, of all things) and the skels seemed to stop making as much noise. Grit also stopped wailing so much.

And I began to be able to move. Not all at once, and I had to fight myself to do it, but I was slowly starting to get up.

Grit and I were on our knees at about the same time. I nodded to her and her back to me. Then I looked to see Karrish in a tug of war with a wolf for the Staff of Orcus. I don't know Orcus and hope to never meet him, but I don't think that the Lord of the Underworld would be very pleased that his servant was failing because of not being able to defeat, as Karrish put it, a mutt.

Then I saw it. The ruby stone at the top of the staff glowed. It burnt a deep, dark reddish hue, and I saw Grit turn her head to avoid looking at it. The chasm began to glow the same hue, and something was groaning from within it.

The intensity grew, along with the moaning, and the ground began to shake. I jumped to Grit and covered her with (what I had of) a body and cloak. I braced for it.

The skels who had stopped had no protection. Neither did Grimmaw nor the other two. The blast from the staff pushed me and Grit to the edge of the cliff that I had climbed. My left arm detached again and was holding on for dear life. I caught Grit with my other. Everything, for the moment, was silent.

Then the moaning from below grew, and Karrish laughed. Grit climbed up beside me and we both looked at the necromancer and the destruction he had wrought. Grimmaw, Alleron, and Brigid were laying, awkwardly, against the far wall of the cavern; I was not sure if they were still alive. The skels who fought for Karrish were blown apart. Grit screamed and charged.

I heard myself say "No!" to her, but it was far too late. A red bolt launched from the ruby and struck her. She fell, twitching. Alive, maybe barely, but in a seizure.

"I will deal with these others later, but time grows long." Karrish was walking towards me now, "I must complete the prayer." Another loud moan came from below. It seemed closer now. Stronger.

The ruby glowed again as he picked up his grimoire and righted the podium that it had been on. I went to attack him. The ruby seemed to sense this and said, "Halt."

I halted.

The rock seemed to look at me, deep into me, through me. I could not resist its command.

Karrish continued with his prayer, oblivious to me. I felt what I could only describe as a burning sensation throughout my being and then a pulling. Not pulling my body, but my soul. And I felt it leaving me. He, or the Orcus guy, was stealing my life force.

I looked at my friends who had tried to save me from this fate. I should have listened to them and ran. Maybe it would merely have just delayed my fate, but maybe my friends would not have suffered as much.

When I remembered my left arm, I was probably quite close to being too late. I also thought that it would not work, the ruby would sense it. Then I thought, 'What the Hells could I lose at this point?' I thought that I may get slapped across the face by my own hand, which would have been embarrassing, but still better than just letting this traitor have an eternal life without trying it. Or whatever it was that was moaning, getting out of that chasm.

I moved as if to strike Karrish with my left arm. At first I felt it was going to fail, I did not feel it move. But then I heard the whooshing noise as it flew by my head, straight towards the cleric.

He moved aside and laughed. My arm had missed him.

Then he realized what I had done. It was not him that my arm was targeting. It turned at the last moment and struck the ruby. The staff setting broke, and the ruby fell from it. My left hand came back and caught it. Karrish dove to take it from my hand, but my hand was too quick. It threw the ruby over the cliff towards the city of the dead.

By then I was free and moving towards him. He called for his pain spell, which unfortunately still worked, but less so than before, and I grabbed his staff with my right hand. My left returned to where it should be and we wrestled for the staff.

He kept chanting as we fell, though the pain was endurable and the moaning decreased. He ended up on top of me and smashed me with the broken staff. My grip weakened, and he pulled, rising to his knees above me.

He raised the staff. I watched as the cleric's face distorted in rage and the staff began to lower towards my skull.

I would have closed my eyes if I could, but I watched it descend.

Then stopped.

A skel sword swung up and deflected the blow. Karrish rolled towards the chasm's edge. Grit swung at him ferociously, pushing him back. He blocked each blow, but her anger fueled blows kept driving him back.

One relieved him of the staff, and he fell to the ground. She kept her attack, screaming with every blow as the cleric rolled away. He was on the edge.

I walked to them and picked up the Staff of Orcus, without the ruby and put my hand on Grit's shoulder. The cleric looked at us and uttered a weak, "please, help..." before a giant hand reached up and took him, nearly taking us with him.

~

The others were alive, wounded, but nothing permanent physically. The skels were, I'm not sure what to say, but back to being just skeletons. I'm not entirely sure of their ultimate fate, but they seemed to be just regularly dead at that point.

I hoped they were now resting and not seeing what was going on around them, unable to interact.

My fear was that I did not perish, so they did not as well. I grabbed the grimoire and kept the staff, hoping I could find answers. I did not know of Karrish's fate, but we searched the city and never found the ruby. We may meet again some day. That day, I may be much more prepared for the challenge.

The army that attacked the goblins and humans stopped attacking at some point, and then just fell where they had stood. We were told of the horrors that the survivors had faced.

I did not envy their struggle. I hoped that, at the very least, they could coexist beyond this.

Chapter 25

My Toe

I stayed about a week or so, helping to clean up. Fix up the human town and the goblin village. Bury the skels, the humans, and goblins. There were so many. It was gruesome work, but it kept my mind busy, which was what I needed.

I visited with my daughter, which was awkward, but nice.

And Grit and Grimmaw. We would go to where I once thought of living a peaceful, not-so-dead life, helping to watch over the wolves. We played throw the stick and bring it back many times. The wolf was always appreciative until he wasn't and would just lie down and make me go get the stick. It was fun, but not the same.

Grit asked me to stay. So did the Grandfather and surprisingly, Zrakkon.

I said that I would think about it, but I already knew.

I could not stay so close to my wife and her new (new being a relative term as compared to me) husband.

I did not blame her one bit, but it still hurt to see them. I visited with them once, and if I thought the visits with my daughter were awkward, those were beyond. When I said goodbye after, I knew then that it was a permanent, or as permanent as possible, goodbye.

Alleron stayed with me for the most part. He said he could not leave until his debt was repaid. I told him he was forgiven, and that he had repaid it more than a few times. But, I feel he, like me, could not find a place to fit in.

I hated to admit it; but I liked his company. He reminded me of the times we had adventuring. This was the only times I saw him happy, when he was talking about our old group going out and finding trouble. We did not mention Karrish much when we regaled each other with our memories. I am pretty sure that he may have been exaggerating his accomplishments on more than one occasion, but I did not call him on it.

He helped me learn to read the book. More than once I saw the greed in his eyes as I put it away into my pack, but never did he try to take it or even ask. He just helped me. Hopefully, it will help me understand what is going on with me.

Grit, Grimmaw, Brigid, and I buried what we hoped would be the final body. "I think that's it." I said, after packing the last of the dirt on top.

"It's too bad no one will ever know exactly where their family is buried," Grit said. Brigid pulled her in close.

"It is," I said. I wanted to say more, something that would lift up her spirits. Nothing came to mind.

Instead, of course, I said the stupidest thing I could at that moment. "I think that I need to leave."

"The cemetery?" Brigid asked, attempting to get me to change the subject.

I missed it completely. "No, this place. I don't fit anywhere here. Maybe anywhere. Karrish may be out there somewhere. And I need to figure out this book and find out how to..."

"Die," Grit said softly. I now figured out what Brigid meant. If I had not, the look on the blonde woman's face would have told me exactly how badly I messed up at that moment. Her face did not really have to though. Grit's did that job perfectly.

She then ran off, Grimmaw following faithfully behind her.

"Well, that could have gone better." Brigid told me, "I'm coming with you, you know?"

"I figured as much."

"I am going to leave," I told Alleron when I got back to the wolves' den (That's what we had decided to call it when we got back, seemed to have a bit of a ring to it.)

"Of course," he said, "I'm already packed."

It seemed like everyone knew that I would be leaving besides me and Grit. "You don't have to come. Your debt has been forgiven."

"Maybe to you, my lord." Was all he said. I wanted to say more, to tell him how helping me when he did not need to, in watching over the wolf and the girl had paid his debt. How his helping to save Grit, meant the world to me and repaid what had been dealt in my lifetime twofold. He, of course, would not listen to that nonsense. He needed to see me content. To see me know what my fate would be. Plus, I had told him all this already. "I already told everyone. They're going to meet us at the town square."

"Goblins too?" I asked.

"Goblins too," said Alleron, "they are actually getting along quite well."

"For now. I give it a couple of weeks." Brigid added.

"Hopefully, they can at least find a way to coexist." I said, and we headed to the town.

Everyone, save one, was there. I talked with my daughter, I explained, and she accepted that I did not belong there.

I talked with my (I don't want to say ex, as that has negative connotations, former wife, maybe) and she, too, understood my decision. She actually seemed quite relieved. I can't say that I blamed her. Her husband smiled at me. I actually liked him, which seemed quite odd. But he was a good guy.

I walked to the Grandfather and shook his hand, the way the goblins did. He said thank you, and then something in his language. I took it to mean good luck and farewell. It seemed appropriate.

Even Zrakkon was there. But the one that I wanted to see was not. Maybe the two.

The wolf and the girl ended up coming together as we made our goodbyes. The goblin girl riding the wolf came up to me and said, quite frankly, "We're coming."

"As long as your grandfather ..." I started.

"He said you would protect me." she looked at me in my eye sockets, "will you?"

"Of course," I said.

"Then we're coming too," and I welcomed them. The five of us, the blonde, the mage, the dead, the goblin, and the wolf, trying to find our way. There would be many journeys ahead.

But, even with Grit and Grimmaw with us, something was missing. "Where are you going?" Brigid asked as I started back toward the Wolves' Den.

"I need to find my toe." I said and kept walking.

I walked along the perimeter, and I felt for it. I wiggled it. And I found it. I reached down into the tall grass where it lay, my middle toe. I picked it up as the others watched and I placed it where it should be. It attached and completed my body. I was whole again.

I looked to where Odem's hut had been and reminisced for a moment. I wondered what could have been. I took that in. I needed to.

In a simpler world, I probably would not exist. I would have remained dead in my cavern and rested with the others. But, in another, another world, I may have simply sat in Odem's hut and watched the wolves. And protected them.

And been content in doing so.

www.ingramcontent.com/pod-product-compliance
Lightning Source LLC
Chambersburg PA
CBHW050333110726
47899CB00007B/2487